All the Dirty Cowards

A JESUS CREEK MYSTERY

Deborah Adams

This book is a work of fiction. All names, characters, places, and events are the product of the author's imagination. References to Jesse James and J. D. Howard as characters in the story are fictitious. Any resemblance to actual events or persons, living or dead, is entirely coincidental and beyond the intent of either the author or the publisher.

Hardcover ISBN 1-57072-115-7
Trade Paper ISBN 1-57072-131-9
Copyright © 2000 by Deborah Adams
Printed in the United States of America
All Rights Reserved

1 2 3 4 5 6 7 8 9 0

This book is dedicated to Thea Chalecky,
the lady who made it happen.

Many thanks to the folks who helped with research for this book: Lydia Corbett, Don Donaldson, Patrick V. Garland, Justine P. Honeyman, David Hunter, Thurston James, D. D. Maddox, Sharyn McCrumb, Larry McKee, Grady Patrick Jr., Ed Price, Dr. Kevin Smith, Elizabeth Daniels Squire, Dr. Jim Veatch, and Fran Wheatley.

CAST OF CHARACTERS, THEN

Delia Cannon I: Ancestress of Delia the sleuth. The original Ms. Cannon owned Jesus Creek's first saloon. Her business was highly successful.

J. D. Howard/Rabbit Man: A grain dealer and horseman from a nearby community, Mr. Howard often visited Jesus Creek on business.

Clarissa Turner: Every story needs a pretty girl. Clarissa fulfills the requirement in this one.

Mary Turner: Clarissa's less attractive but serious-minded sister makes for balance in the Turner family.

Mrs. Turner: Yet another successful businesswoman, Mrs. Turner opens her home to boarders and is mother to both Clarissa and Mary.

Jeremiah Vickers: Recently arrived from the Boston area, Jeremiah is Jesus Creek's new schoolteacher. He will undoubtedly be changed by his experiences on the wild frontier.

Elmer Winter: Ancestor to Miss Constance, Elmer is a wise prophet. Either that or he's just plain nuts.

CAST OF CHARACTERS, NOW

Delia Cannon II: Descended from Delia I, our sleuth is a worthy successor to the name.

Eloise: Owner of the town's favorite diner, Eloise's tongue was the original information superhighway.

Reb Gassler: The Jesus Creek Police Chief, he is completely oblivious to his family history.

Lenny Hemby: By all accounts, Lenny is a good guy with the misfortune of being raised in a household of women.

Lodina Hemby Lane: Lenny's sister is recently divorced (not her fault). She is a friend and next-door neighbor to Delia II.

Sarah Elizabeth Leach: The town's librarian, Sarah Elizabeth is a relative newcomer to Jesus Creek, but she tries hard to fit in.

Kay Martin: The only female member of the Jesus Creek Police Department, Kay brings her own special talents to the job.

Dan McClain: Dan is the most recent addition to the Jesus Creek family. Little is known about him, but it's only a matter of time before Eloise takes care of that.

Fern Oatley: The state forensic investigator, Ms. Oatley is a fan of Nashville's hockey team, the Predators.

Patricia Patrick: An attractive, mature woman, Patricia has a lot to offer the right man.

Roger Shelton: Roger is the crazy Yankee who loves and is loved by Delia II.

Constance Winter: Elmer's descendant, Miss Constance pretty much sets the tone for the town, even though she is currently a resident of the Jesus Creek Nursing Home.

A helpful suggestion from the author:
If you don't find a character listed here, it probably means that character is only passing through and will have no major role in the story. Try not to think too much about it.

Memoirs of Jeremiah Vickers, loose manuscript, page 1 (now part of a mouse nest in the attic of the Vickers home)

I am dying. I know it, even though the doctor continues in his blustery effort to persuade me otherwise. I see it in his florid face; I see it in the eyes of my wife when she brings my meals or sits knitting by my bedside; I see it in the mirror when I shave.

Worst of all, I see death in the blazing eyes of the spectre that comes every night to taunt me with the certain knowledge that my soul is bound for hell.

CHAPTER ONE

DOT VICKERS DECLINED along with her sagging Victorian farmhouse for over forty years before a broken hip forced her to relocate to the Jesus Creek Nursing Home. She resided there in steadily decreasing health for nearly a year, finally succumbing to the inevitable.

A month later, on a surprisingly warm January day, the old Vickers house and all its contents went up for auction, and as was the way in Jesus Creek, Tennessee, the town turned out for the festivities. Discussion of The Stranger was an unexpected bonus.

Dot had been a thirty-something widow when she married Pete Vickers and moved into his home. That had been in the early 1950s. Now Pete was long gone and Dot's children were long grown.

Lenny Hemby and Lodina Hemby Lane, products of Dot's first marriage to Horace Hemby, watched from a corner of the yard as the auctioneer offered up stained doilies, worn-out ladder-back chairs, and truckloads of rotting antiques and rusted collectibles. The bidding for such kitsch as plastic window curtains and donkey condiment sets was fast and furious, as well. Lodina and Lenny would make a tidy profit from the garbage their mother had not bothered to throw away.

The house and land would be the final sale of the day, although it seemed unlikely that anyone would want to buy it at any price. Just west of town, the Vickers house had been solidly built in the days when a craftsman's pride meant everything. It was never sufficiently grand to meet the standards of upper-class Victorians, but once upon a time the house had boasted a three-sided covered porch and enough gingerbread to make any farmwife proud.

Dot Vickers, though, had been a twentieth-century woman, alone for a long time and unable to keep up with even basic maintenance, much less repair. The old place was in need of paint, a new roof, and many thousands of dollars worth of restoration.

In the yard, dead trees vied for space with scrub brush that crept closer to the house every growing season. Out back, a stone's throw from the rotting porch, the barn leaned thirty degrees off-plumb, just waiting for a strong wind to put it out of its misery.

Delia Cannon loved history and she hoped whoever bought the Vickers farm would restore the house to its former glory. All the same, she thanked her lucky stars that chore didn't fall to her.

Keeping a close eye on the bidding, she still managed to follow the path of the stranger. He'd been there early, already roaming the yard and casually digging through boxes when Delia arrived at eight that morning.

"Who is that?"

Everyone asked; no one knew. The gray-haired gentleman with the handsome, if craggy, face gave them no clues. Oh, he exchanged pleasantries with this one, chatted about the weather with that one—if the other spoke first—but he divulged neither his name nor his reason for attending the estate sale in Jesus Creek, Tennessee.

Aside from whispered conversation about the stranger, the locals who were present for the auction were kept busy commenting on the items up for bid and watching their neighbors buy largely worthless junk at rock-bottom prices. Every so often, a sense of guilt would sweep over the crowd, reminding them that they were, essentially, vultures pecking away at the bones of Dot Vickers's life.

To Delia Cannon's delight, the old woman had saved every scrap of paper she'd ever run across, stashing them in boxes and bags with no noticeable plan or method. For an amateur genealogist and historian like Delia, the apparent trash was truly treasure and it was her good fortune to be the only person at the auction willing to bid on the musty trunk full of letters, ledgers, and outdated legal documents.

"You couldn't have gotten a nice yard ornament?" Roger Shelton, Delia's longtime significant other, complained as he hefted the massive trunk into the back of her small car.

"I was hoping for the broken flamingos," Delia admitted, "but the price was too high and the color clashes with my dead grass." She tied down the hatchback with a rope she'd brought along for just that purpose. "There's no telling what's in this trunk," she added. "Could be a pirate's treasure. Better still, it could be a family Bible!"

"And what would a pagan such as yourself do with that?" Roger asked.

Before Delia could explain the importance of the find to an amateur genealogist, they were joined by Sarah Elizabeth Leach. "Look what I got!" Sarah Elizabeth exclaimed.

Reb Gassler followed along behind her, patiently carrying a box crammed full of tattered books. "She blew ten bucks on this," he said to Roger, who understood and sympathized.

"Look at this one, Delia," Sarah Elizabeth went on. She pulled a blue clothbound book from her oversized bag. "*The Moonstone,* by Wilkie Collins!"

"You're kidding." Delia inspected the book carefully, then nodded approvingly. "I don't know anything about collectible books, but this may be valuable. Don't put it on the library shelves."

Sarah Elizabeth shook her head. "It's a mystery, right? I'll ask the book discussion group. One of them is sure to know all about it."

"Sarah Elizabeth, could you just tell me where you want these so I can put 'em down?" Reb asked with long-suffering patience.

"Oh, I'm sorry. Delia, I have to drive Reb back to town. You're staying for the big event, right?"

"I wouldn't miss it!" Delia promised. "Y'all go on. I'll catch up with you later."

Roger gave Reb a look of male understanding. "I'll be stuck

here all day, too," he said, "unless you need me in town for something. Maybe you want to interrogate me? I'll pretty much confess to anything if it'll get me out of here."

"You want to get me on Delia's bad side?" Reb asked as he trudged away with Sarah Elizabeth's books. "No way! I'd rather wrassle Hulk Hogan. Consider yourself officially pardoned for whatever crimes you've committed."

Roger sighed. "You'd think an officer of the law would be tougher than that."

Dinner on the ground usually referred to a church event, but in Jesus Creek any excuse for a community picnic was enthusiastically embraced. Trina's Tea Room offered watercress and cucumber sandwiches from the concession booth, along with fresh fruit and vegetable trays.

For the hearty eaters, Eloise's Diner had sent over massive quantities of beef sandwiches and greasy fries. Offering a little something for everyone, the concession booth was doing a brisk business during the noon lunch break when Delia and Roger joined the queue.

"Who is that handsome man?" Patricia Patrick whispered. She nodded once in the direction of the house, where the gray-haired stranger stood calmly inspecting the crowd on the lawn.

Delia cast a casual glance across the heads of the milling crowd. "No one seems to know who he is," she said. "He's been here all day, though, just roaming around. Could be he's with Lenny and Lodina. Or maybe he came with the auctioneer."

Patricia shook her head briskly. "Nope. And no one knows why he's here. Now I just think that's peculiar." She pursed her lips in bewilderment.

"Possibly," Roger said thoughtfully, "he's a junk collector here to replenish his stock."

Delia and Patricia ignored the suggestion.

"Here's Lodina and Lenny," Patricia said as Dot's heirs joined them in the concession line, temporarily increasing the awkwardness of the day.

"The sale's going well, don't you think?" Delia said tactfully.

"Yes," Lodina agreed, adjusting her gray-but-stylishly-coiffed hair. "Lenny started out keeping a tally but he's already lost interest in that." She laughed and ruffled her brother's hair as if Lenny's short attention span were a joke.

"I saw him jotting notes. It's a good idea," Delia said. "Not that you can't trust your auctioneer, but just in case someone misplaces a decimal."

"That's exactly what I thought," Lenny said with a grin. "But I decided I'd risk losing a few dollars after I found out keeping track of all those numbers bored me to tears. I pity the clerk who's got the job. I'd sure hate to do this for a living, especially if I worked on commission."

Lodina nodded. "Mama's junk doesn't amount to much anyway. Poor old thing spent her whole life accumulating the bare necessities. She never had anything nice. It's a real shame."

"Oh, but honey," Patricia said as she patted Lodina's arm, "she had a good long life, and now she's at peace. That's the best any of us can hope for."

Lodina's eyes threatened to well with tears, but Lenny merely gazed off into the distance. "When I was a young'un," he said to no one in particular, "I used to camp out in those woods back there behind the barn. Built my shelter with limbs and twigs. Caught rabbits in traps I made myself, and cooked 'em over an open fire. Kids nowadays don't know what self-reliance means." The sadness in his voice could have been for deprived modern youth, or for his own distant childhood.

Lacking interest in Lenny's nostalgia, Patricia pointed to the stranger who was ambling around the property as if he'd merely strolled into the crowd by accident. "Lodina, who is that? I know I've never seen him before, and he hasn't bid on a single thing all morning."

Lodina shrugged. "No telling. There's a bunch of people here with no intention of buying anything. He's probably just another gawker."

Lenny studied the unknown man for a moment but offered

no guess about his identity. "You know, I think I'll just take one last walk through those woods," he said and sauntered away.

Patricia grabbed Lodina's elbow. "He's got a good idea," she said. "It's time to say a proper good-bye. Come on, honey. I'll go through the house with you and we'll just bid it a good farewell."

"I really don't—" Lodina began, but Patricia shushed her.

"Now it'll be good for you to get it out of your system. I've got a box full of Kleenex in my bag. You just enjoy the memories and let the tears come." Patricia dragged Lodina across the yard and into the old homeplace, determined to help Lodina find closure, whether she wanted it or not.

This left Delia and Roger alone to enjoy their lunches. "Let's sit over there," Delia said, indicating a sheltered spot beside a run of scrub bushes. She grabbed a few paper napkins from the holder and stuffed them in her lunch sack before they headed across the yard.

"Lodina's doing well," Delia announced, as soon as they'd seated themselves on someone's deserted lawn chairs and unwrapped their food.

"Has she been sick?" Roger asked.

"No, I mean after the divorce," Delia reminded him. "It must have been hard for her to get past Jim dumping her for that. . . ."

"Floozy?" Roger offered. "Hussy? Tramp?"

"It's not for us to judge," she said with her eyes cast toward the cloud-obscured heavens, "but those are all accurate descriptions."

"Did you give Lodina the pep talk?" Roger asked and bit a chunk out of his burger. "Tell her how wonderful your new life is? Now that you have me, I mean." Mustard had squished out of the bun and dripped down his chin.

Delia leaned over to wipe his face with a napkin and give him a peck on the cheek. "Why bother? No ordinary human could possibly understand how much joy you've brought to my life."

This unexpected admission left Roger speechless, but only

for a moment. "Feel free to say that very thing to Lodina. Or to anyone else you run into," he said. "Sometimes—I know this is crazy—but sometimes I get the feeling your friends don't like me."

"They're just scared of you, dear," Delia assured him. "And well they should be."

She would have enumerated the antics that had created his reputation, but she knew all too well that it was pointless; Roger considered himself a fun-loving bon vivant, and no amount of explanation could make him understand that he was justifiably known around Jesus Creek as a trouble-maker—and a Yankee, to boot.

"Besides," she went on, "Lodina's situation isn't like mine. She was the dump*ee*, not the dump*er*. That's much more traumatic, you know. And she's got to be almost seventy, don't you think? Not the time of life when you expect to be divorced."

"I guess it might've ruined her plans," Roger allowed. "Then again, maybe she's just been waiting for a chance to start over."

"Look at that," Delia said, pointing toward the barn behind the Vickers house. "Lenny's following that guy, the one nobody knows."

"Following?" Roger asked skeptically. "Or just walking behind him in the same direction?"

"Hmmm." Delia watched as Lenny gained ground and finally got close enough to the stranger to tap him on the shoulder. It seemed to her that the man turned to face Lenny as if he'd been expecting him, anticipating the moment. They were too far away, of course, for Delia to hear the conversation, but if facial expressions and body language meant anything at all, the two men did not form an instant friendship.

"I wonder what that's about," she mused.

"Go ask," Roger suggested.

"It's none of my business," Delia replied, as if he'd brought it up himself. "Besides, I'd rather spend my lunch break examining that trunk I bought. Come on. Let's see if I've found Blackbeard's gold!"

"At least you've got something to burn in the woodstove this winter," Roger conceded after he'd watched her unpack half the trunk.

"It's probably nothing worth saving," Delia admitted. "On the other hand, some of those papers might be of historical interest."

"You can't even balance your checkbook," Roger argued. "Okay, maybe you could do it if you'd ever tried it. You have no idea where you put the good silver; your car hasn't had an oil change in its life; and frankly, I'm worried about the dog. He hasn't been seen in weeks."

"I don't have a dog," she reminded him.

"The point is, you won't spend ten minutes organizing the necessities of life, but you'll devote months to reading, copying, and filing this bunch of"—he picked up a newspaper clipping from the top of the pile—"recipes for Co-Cola Salad."

"If you'd examine it carefully," Delia said, taking the yellowed clipping from his hand and turning it over, "you'd see that, on the other side, there's an article about Pope Pius XII naming twenty-four new cardinals."

"And this is important—why?"

"Because only one was American. Francis McIntyre." She gently put the brittle clipping back in the trunk. "It may not matter to you, but news then is history now. It has to be preserved."

"So in forty or fifty years," he said, "someone will be interested in learning that Roger Shelton, innocent bystander and loyal flunky, died of starvation while his significant other waxed poetic over—"

"Don't be silly, man," she said firmly. "No one will be the least bit interested in what became of you. Now keep digging!"

Numerous complaints from Roger later, Delia struck gold in the bottom of the nest-makings. It wasn't the family Bible or packet of Civil War-era letters she'd hoped to run across, but something potentially better—a manuscript of Jeremiah Vickers's memoirs!

"And you said all this was a waste of money!" Delia held

the yellowed pages tenderly. "I can't believe the luck. Just look, Roger!"

"Whoo-eee," Roger said snidely. "Wouldja look at that! There's something you don't see everyday—antique toilet paper."

Ignoring him, Delia gently thumbed through the pages. "Darn it all! There's a bunch missing from the beginning. It looks like the story picks up just when he got to Jesus Creek, though, so that should be useful."

"Is this someone you know?" Roger asked. He realized, of course, that the author of the memoirs had been dead for years, possibly decades, but Delia's relationship with her ancestors transcended the veil. More than once Roger had listened to fascinating tales of tomfoolery and passion, only to discover that the protagonists had perished sometime before the wheel was invented.

"I'm not sure exactly how he fits," Delia said thoughtfully, "but his name is Vickers and this trunk came from the Vickers house. Ergo, he must be part of that family. Of course, none of the Vickers line is still alive, at least not in these parts. Dot Vickers just married a Vickers—she wasn't actually a Vickers herself—and I don't know what became of the Vickers she married, but so far as I know he has no descendants. I don't believe we have another branch of the family living around here. I'll have to find out. . . ."

Roger let her ramble on. He knew she wasn't really talking to him anyway, and Delia knew Roger knew. She considered it a sign of a healthy relationship. He thought of it as a perfectly normal male-female conversation.

"This is a great way to break in your Christmas gift," Roger said, suddenly more enthused about her purchase. "You can use it to organize your newspaper clippings!"

The gift he referred to was the computer he'd foisted upon her, in the firm but mistaken belief that Delia wanted to share his obsession. For over a month, the blasted thing had been parked in the middle of her dining room table, with cords and cables running all over the floor. Roger kept threatening to teach her how to use it. Delia knew she couldn't put it off forever, but she intended to delay it as long as possible.

"Oh, look," she said. "The auction's starting up again. Let's get back over there before we miss a bargain."

As the auction resumed, Delia reluctantly tore herself away from the treasure chest and rejoined the crowd in the front yard. Nothing else among the offerings caught her eye, possibly because her attention was fixed on the stranger who had taken up his position directly in front of the auctioneer.

The man had given no indication of his reason for attending, and he'd bid on nothing—until the final sale of the day, when the mysterious stranger purchased, for the starting amount and without competition, the Vickers house and property.

Delia was posted at her living room window, determined to catch her next-door neighbor the instant Lodina returned home. If there was one thing Delia Cannon hated above all others, it was an unsolved mystery.

"Someone's going to mistake you for Frankie Mae!" Roger called from the dining room.

"Hush, and swim the Internet!" she shouted back.

The man had been sitting at that computer ever since they'd returned from the auction. In Delia's opinion, all computers should be demolished. Not only did they promote those dreadful situations she'd read about in the paper, they encouraged her to use foul language every time she tripped over the cords and cables in her combination kitchen and dining room.

"She's here!" Delia cried as Lenny's car pulled into his sister's driveway. "I'm going over to say hello."

"You're going over to snoop," Roger muttered.

Grabbing the jacket she'd stashed by the door, Delia hurried outside and across the yard to Lodina's house. "Hey, you two!"

Lenny and Lodina didn't seem the least bit surprised to see her. They both waved as Delia joined them beside Lenny's car.

Even a stranger to Jesus Creek could see these two were brother and sister. Both were tall and lean, Lodina's head coming as far as Lenny's nose. Both had thick silvery hair that complemented their rosy complexions, and the bone structure they shared gave them clean, firm profiles.

They may have been raised by poor dirt farmers, Delia thought, but to look at them, anyone would assume they'd grown up in Monaco's royal family.

"We don't know who he is," Lodina said before Delia could ask.

"You don't?" Crestfallen, Delia looked to Lenny for more information. "But I saw you talking to him."

Lenny's face broke into a good-natured grin. "I'm as curious as the rest of you," he admitted. "Saw him roaming around, and he looked familiar. For the life of me, I can't figure out why. So I just went up and introduced myself, thinking he might be bashful about speaking first."

"At our age," Lodina said, "most everybody looks familiar, and people overlook it if we can't put a name to a face."

Delia chuckled. "Well, I can tell you he didn't look a bit familiar to me. Or maybe I'm farther gone than you and can't even remember faces. Did he know you, Lenny?"

For a second Lenny's face went slack, as if the question took him by surprise. Then he shook his head. "No, he didn't. Guess he's just got one of those faces."

"The important thing," Lodina said, "is that he's got one of those checkbooks."

Yes, that much Delia had concluded merely from the stranger's demeanor. He was a man without financial worry. Or an excellent actor, one who internalized the role of wealthy investor. "Surely you got a name," she prodded.

"Daniel McClain," Lodina said quickly. "Not a name I've ever heard. You?"

"No," Delia said, "and I don't believe we have any McClains around here. I wonder why he bought the place. He sure as heck didn't stop just because he saw the AUCTION signs. That man came out today specifically to buy your farm."

"Thank goodness he did!" Lodina rolled her eyes. "Nobody

else would've bought the place. There wasn't a single bid besides his."

Lenny took his sister's arm, a sign that he was ready to end the conversation and get out of the icy air.

"I don't know but what we'd all've been better off if that old place had burned to the ground," he said. "This man—this McClain. He's not very friendly. I wouldn't be surprised if he comes in here and stirs up trouble."

Looking up at her brother, Lodina asked, "What makes you say that, Lenny? What did the two of you talk about?"

Delia was now more curious than ever. Daniel McClain must have set a record for rudeness if he'd made such a poor impression on Lenny that quickly.

Lenny took a few steps toward the side door of Lodina's house. "Nothing in particular," he said. "There's just something about him that sets me off. You about ready to eat?"

"Don't let me keep you from Lodina's good cooking," Delia said, even though she'd have preferred to interrogate Lenny a while longer. "And don't worry about Mr. McClain. Any trouble he can think of to cause, Roger's already on top of."

CHAPTER TWO

DELIA WAS SAVED from her first computer lesson by extraterrestrial beings. Nothing, not even his beloved Internet,
kept Roger Shelton away from the weekly meeting of his
favorite social club, the Universal Friends Organization—
UFO, for short.

He'd worked his way up through the ranks by creating a
position he was uniquely qualified to fill (chairman of the
Alien Sign Tracking committee) and then by encouraging the
UFO President, Henry Mooten, in his increasingly bizarre
notions about the need for an extraterrestrial craft landing
pad in Jesus Creek. This was not a secret organization; in
fact, they held regular fund-raisers to which the public was
invited. So why, Delia wondered, didn't anyone suggest that
Henry Mooten might be a little too far around the bend to
serve as the town's mayor?

There was one other thing that puzzled her: why hadn't
anyone in the organization asked Roger if he had ever seen or
even believed in the space aliens his organization wanted to
welcome? Roger was a troublemaker and an agitator, but he
was—in his own convoluted way—both honest and ethical.
If asked outright, he'd answer truthfully, and then he'd be
promptly stripped of his title and expelled unceremoniously
from UFO.

At least Delia had the solution to one mystery; the Vickers farm now belonged to Daniel McClain, a man with no
known connections to Jesus Creek, no imaginable reason
for wanting the property, and no apparent desire to explain
himself to his new neighbors.

Delia was not concerned by her current lack of information. After all, piecing together life histories was her specialty and her passion. True, she usually tracked dead people, but it would be easier to trace the living, wouldn't it? She was confident that Daniel McClain would be an open book to her in no time.

At the moment, however, she was much more interested in exploring another book—*The Memoirs of Jeremiah Vickers*, or what remained of it.

After a hot shower, Delia stocked her favorite reading nook with cookies, coffee, and one of Pam Satterfield's knitted afghans. She dug the memoirs from the trunk which Roger had grudgingly helped her move to the middle of her living room floor, then stretched out on the sofa and gave her full attention to the Victorian gentleman who had so graciously provided her with the first tantalizing clues in a new mystery.

The paper was remarkably well preserved, the ink still clear, and the handwriting an excellent example of nineteenth century penmanship. The manuscript seemed sturdy enough to hold up through careful readings. Delia would type a copy later, to add to the genealogy section at the Jesus Creek Public Library; for the moment, though, she wanted to savor every word of the neatly penned tale.

As she read, the historian in her deeply regretted that so much of the first section had been lost, and it horrified her to see that sections of what remained were stained. Given the nibble marks around the edges of several pages, she preferred not to think of what had caused those stains, but she'd certainly wash her hands well before touching her snacks!

It was a miracle, really, that any of the manuscript survived. Delia guessed that the trunk might have belonged to Jeremiah Vickers, for his memoirs were at the very bottom. If the Vickers clan had run their attic the same way Delia ran hers, that trunk had served as a convenient place to store odds and ends throughout the years. Judging by the broad range of dates on the documents she'd found atop the manuscript, it was likely to have been a storehouse for more than one generation.

I wonder if anyone else ever read these memoirs, she

thought. It gave her a thrill to imagine that she was the first to share Jeremiah's life story.

Memoirs of Jeremiah Vickers, chapter 7, page 103

Shortly afterward, I found myself en route to my new home on the frontier, where I had been engaged to teach at a small but ambitious school. Accustomed as I was to the mild and ordinary lifestyle of a quiet Eastern village, I naturally found the thriving town of Jesus Creek intimidating.

Though primitive in aspect, the businesses already in existence included a postal office, a general goods store, an elegantly fronted bank, and the requisite stables and smiths, in addition to the furniture and mortuary store.

Several people hurried about with purpose, completing business or chores, while others gathered briefly in small forums to exchange news and pleasantries. Wagons traveled the main street at regular intervals, the rhythmic clicking of hooves setting a beat for the joyous cries of small children. Not even the high temperature produced by afternoon sun diminished the lively atmosphere.

"What life!" I said to the others in my coach. "What boundless energy! Imagine the future as this town grows toward its destiny."

As soon as the driver halted his team in the heart of the bustling main street, my fellow travelers disappeared behind the broad door of Delia's Tavern, a lager saloon that appeared to be a popular gathering place for saint and sinner alike. Stifling summer heat and the dust of the road conspired to cause me a moment's hesitation. It wouldn't be so bad, I thought, if I stepped inside for a cool drink of water. Good sense prevailed, however, and I reluctantly admitted that a man of my position ought not to be seen in such a place.

A small boy stood near the tavern's hitching post, drawing circles in the dust with his bare toes while holding tight to the reins of a magnificent sorrel horse.

"Why not tie him, boy?" I asked. "And free yourself for some amusement?"

"Man paid me a penny," the urchin replied without

elaboration.

It was not my concern, of course, but having been raised to appreciate the virtue of frugality, I found such a habit wasteful. I had approached the boy with the intention of asking directions, but at that moment the saloon's door was thrown open and out stumbled a perfect example of the dangers of excess.

Leaning against the post to steady himself, the grizzled old-timer, fragrant with gin, caught sight of me and grinned, exposing a row of exquisitely well-formed teeth. "Must be the schoolmarm," he pronounced.

"Master," I corrected and reluctantly put forth a hand in greeting. "Schoolmaster. May I ask how you recognized me, sir?"

Ignoring my gesture, the pitiful soul spat a stream of snuff into the road. "Who else but a 'ristocrat would come dressed like that?" Then, turning to the boy, he asked, "Why doncha tie 'im?"

"Man paid me a penny," the boy said again, but this time he felt compelled to elaborate. "Rabbit Man's a plug-hat gent and I kin use the pay."

"Huhn!" The drunkard spat once more. "That's a rabbit that's done put one over on the hound. Look at that!" He pointed to the very fine saddle strapped to the sorrel, directing our attention in particular to the holsters attached one to either side. "That there's a guerrilla saddle, not some fancy gentleman's seat."

The boy shook his head. "Rabbit Man said he bought it off a man. You know he ain't never touched a gun. He don't even take real drink in there, jus' Miss Delia's lemonade. And he jumps at shadows." Tired of the discussion, the boy took a few steps away from us and offered the horse a drink from the nearest trough.

"Gullible, I reckon." The old man pondered this revelation for a moment. "Now, Schoolmarm," he went on, "you going in for some refreshment, or you just expecting to stand here 'til you freeze?"

The specimen before me, while not of a class one chooses

for one's own, was, nevertheless, a human being worthy of redemption, or so my religion asserted. It occurred to me that, in addition to educating the youth of Jesus Creek, my purpose in this place might well be to help convert such as he to a more civilized style of life, and so I set about this charitable task by addressing him in a manner as polite and sociable as I would have adopted toward a man of God. "Forgive my omission. I am Jeremiah Vickers, and pleased to make your acquaintance, Mr. . . ?"

Instantly I saw reward for my effort, for he straightened his rum-withered body and exhibited such dignity as was left to him. "Winter," he said, offering a hand as I had done earlier. "Elmer Winter. Gentleman of leisure, at your service."

"Perhaps you'll do me the favor of directing me to Mrs. Turner's boardinghouse."

A look of fear passed briefly across his face before Mr. Winter responded, "The boardinghouse, eh? He recommend it?" He jerked one stained thumb in the direction of the sorrel.

"The boy? No, I was given instruction in the letter of employment that arrangements had been made for me at Mrs. Turner's."

"Ah, then." The shiftless man's eyes no longer registered apprehension, but neither did they appear as open as they first had. "Down that away, just below town. You'll find it easy enough, if you look for a big white house with lacy curtains. That's what comes of a household run by women. I daresay you won't mind it, though." He looked me over as if assessing a questionable bargain, then staggered back inside the saloon.

Hiring a man with horse and cart, I saw to the loading of my possessions and we set out for Mrs. Turner's boardinghouse. The bawdy words of a popular tune rang forth from Delia's Tavern and followed us until we had traveled several yards. Most of the passersby nodded amiably, and children stopped their youthful sport to examine my person, no doubt envious of the fashionable duds Mother had provided as a parting gift.

I could not help but feel dizzy, assailed as I was from all

sides by the sounds and smells and sights of this foreign yet exciting place. Jesus Creek, Tennessee, was an example of the burgeoning promise of growth and opportunity so abundant in the country in those days, and I felt blessed to be part of it.

Little did I realize at that time how greatly my physical and spiritual landscape would alter.

Heat and exertion combined to destroy my jaunty mood, and by the time I had reached Mrs. Turner's boardinghouse, assisted in the unloading of my belongings, and explained myself to the landlady, the thrilling adventure before me paled in comparison to the delight of a frosty dipper of water.

With one good look at me, Mrs. Turner instantly abandoned her welcoming chatter and shepherded me to the enclosed well at the back of the house. Hauling up the bucket herself, she offered to direct my trunk to the room set aside for me, then encouraged me to drink my fill. I obeyed without argument.

Upon her return, Mrs. Turner led me to a small but adequate room off the kitchen. "I always lodge the gentlemen on this floor," she said. "You'll find it's nearest to the wellhouse and to the gentlemen's convenience out back of the barn. Now I don't mind you coming and going of a night, or even helping yourself to a bite, but I expect you to tidy up afterward."

"I pride myself on orderliness and responsible behavior," I assured her.

"And I hope you're not an edgy sleeper," she went on, "for my other boarder is often about after dark. He's in this room," she said, pointing to a door on the far side of the kitchen from my own room, "so don't fret if you hear footsteps in the night. It's only Mr. Howard, and he'll not harm you. He's so timid, the folks around here call him Rabbit Man."

The heat of the kitchen stove was like a furnace, but the smells provided by the effort reminded me that I had not eaten in several hours. Sensing my thoughts, Mrs. Turner explained the schedule of her establishment. "Dinner's at eleven-thirty, supper's at five," she told me. "If you're late, you'll have to make do with the remains. And I see it's almost time to be setting the table, so if you'll excuse me." Without further ado, she directed me to my quarters and disappeared, one hoped to set about the task of serving supper.

As soon as the door had closed behind me, I made a closer inspection of the room that was to be my home for the next several months. The single window looked out upon a thriving if small orchard, where pears and apples ripened in the heat of summer. I hoped that Mrs. Turner would prove a neat hand with pie crust, for I had always had a fondness for apple pie.

The room itself was sparsely furnished and this condition suited me, for the inherent clutter of women is a deterrent to mental concentration. With a bed, a chair, a table, and the mirrored wardrobe, I had all the accommodations I would need for comfort.

I removed my coat and arranged it carefully across the ladder-back chair so as not to add to the wrinkles and creases put there by my long journey. Later I would brush away the dust, but for the moment I set about improving the appearance of my person before joining the others for supper.

When I had made myself presentable with the help of a handkerchief dipped in water and judiciously applied to my person, I retraced my steps through to the front parlor, where I found my landlady seated in a cool, shadowy corner, engaged in needlework. Beside her, examining a ledger, was a handsome woman who made the briefest of greeting upon our introduction. "My daughter, Mary," Mrs. Turner said, exhibiting obvious pride in the quiet and comely young woman.

"Hottest summer I can remember," Mrs. Turner went on, and motioned me to a chair near her own.

"I should have known better than to go about in this weather," I admitted.

Mrs. Turner clucked. "A pity you didn't arrive after dark. Or take refreshment in town, as our other lodger is apt to do."

"You needn't fear on that account. I am not inclined to partake of spirits," I informed her. "Were I thus disposed, I should have changed my ways immediately upon meeting your townsman, Mr. Winter."

"What?" Mrs. Turner very nearly dropped her piecing. "You ran into him, did you? Well, don't you worry, Mr. Vickers. That man's every bit as feebleminded as the rest of his family. Why, all those Winters are crazy as little bedbugs, and I wouldn't have a one of 'em in this place. Gives a bad name to the town, if you want to know."

Her strong aversion to the old drunkard reassured me that Mrs. Turner was a discerning and morally admirable woman, and instantly I felt as secure as if I had been in my own mother's home.

"I did feel that he might be of a disturbed mind," I told her. "Seeing such a wretch as he, I was more convinced than ever to avoid the lure of saloons."

"Good for you, Mr. Vickers," said the lady. "It's rare enough to find a man with that much sense."

Feeling suddenly tired out from my exertions, I allowed myself a moment of rest. Anxious as the prospect of a new beginning made me, I nonetheless felt elated to have finally reached the end of my journey.

A sudden light burst upon us and my eyes fluttered open to behold a golden angel, her halo shining brightly around her. Instantly, of course, mental adjustment corrected this flawed impression, and I realized that the angel was but a young lady framed in the open doorway, the blistering afternoon sunshine at her back.

"Oh!" she said and clasped the locket that hung around her delicate throat. Stepping inside, she closed the door behind her, then proceeded to study me as if I were a specimen in a case. "You're the schoolteacher, aren't you? The way Mr. Winter described you, I expected a hideously ugly old maid."

"Clarissa!" Mrs. Turner reprimanded this younger daughter with the tone of one who realizes the effort will do no good, but who feels compelled to effect the pretense for the benefit of her own dignity.

As if to prove my surmise correct, the young lady ignored

her mother's stern gaze and came closer to peer at my face. "Well, you aren't hideously ugly," she decided, "and you're built sturdy enough, but underneath your red cheeks, you're terribly pale. Mr. Winter didn't think you'd get this far without collapse."

"Surely you haven't befriended that person," Miss Turner said without looking up from her accounts.

"Oh, but I ran into him as I was walking, and not to speak would have been frightfully rude," Miss Clarissa pointed out. "Now I must hurry and change my dress before supper. I wouldn't have a gentleman see me like this!"

With all the grace of a Heavenly being, the angel floated up the stairs behind us and disappeared. Since I had already seen her with flushed face and mussed hair, I concluded that she was freshening herself for some other gentleman, perhaps a beau.

"A charming daughter you have," I said, thinking there was no need to dilute my appraisal with commentary on the girl's spirited behavior.

"Oh, yes," Mrs. Turner said grimly. "Draws admirers like a dead horse draws flies, but she hasn't got a lick more sense than a Winter. I blame it on her father. He kept his head in the clouds, too. That's what killed him, you know—stepped in front of a phaeton while musing over some fantastic scheme."

"I'm sorry to hear it," I said, for lack of a more genuine sentiment. While I had given the matter no previous thought, I realized suddenly that I was not inclined to share the intimate details of the Turner family, no matter how willing they were to communicate them.

I determined to make myself scarce before more family history was forthcoming. Stretching to restore circulation in my limbs and thus revive my being, I inadvertently glimpsed Miss Turner, who appeared to be watching me in a most intent manner. This so unnerved me that I opted to forgo further pleasantries and retire immediately for a brief respite.

Miss Clarissa, as might have been expected, was the last to join us at the supper table. By the time she arrived, breathless and giggling her apologies, Mrs. Turner had already adorned the table with brimming bowls of beans, corn, mashed turnips, and fried tomatoes as accompaniment to a finely roasted chicken.

It came as no surprise to me when Mrs. Turner proved herself an excellent cook. Her matronly figure showed just such form as is found in women of domestic talent—that is, she conformed to a size that is somewhat fuller than the accepted ideal, without going beyond the absolute limit of female handsomeness.

Neither of her daughters, alas, appeared likely to inherit the mother's skills. The elder Miss Turner, with her sedate and studious mind and demeanor, likely bore the trait of one who perseveres until a recipe has been cooked to perfection. Skill alone, I have found, is no guarantee of success; Miss Turner's too-slender frame marked her as one who does not savor food, and this particular enjoyment is a necessary ingredient to a tasty meal.

Miss Clarissa's healthy appetite was not balanced with an understanding of precision. She would be one of those higgledy-piggledy cooks who throws in a handful of this, a pinch of that, without ever taking the time to measure, thereby concocting a different dish each time.

It had been my lifelong habit, and the habit of my entire family, to partake of meals in relative silence, this being known to benefit digestion. I soon discovered that such was not the routine at Mrs. Turner's table. As quickly as she stopped her apologies, Miss Clarissa began an animated recitation of her conversation with a store's clerk.

"'But, surely, Mr. Mooten,' I said to him, 'surely you have a bolt of deep blue silk?' Well, and do you think he would have a look? Why, no! He's such a stubborn old man, and here I am without a respectable gown to wear to Ginny Wilson's wedding."

Mr. Howard passed me the turnips with a nod and turned to the discussion of dressmaking materials. "Mrs. Howard has often expressed frustration at the lack of available goods in the area. I fear you both may run away to someplace—oh,

Kansas City, let us say—and settle there only because you enjoy the variety of shops."

The gentleman was more gracious than I, for he willingly engaged in senseless conversation such as this throughout the meal. Perhaps, I concluded, his livelihood requires dealings with many strangers, and thus he has learned to carry on in this fashion.

I had not yet learned what business Mr. Howard engaged in, but his appearance suggested that he profited quite well. His brown cashmere suit was surely an expense! Furthermore, his full-face whiskers of dark brown were well-kept, in the manner of gentlemen who have leisure for tending to such vanities.

I considered asking why he wore gloves at the supper table but declined the action, fearing that it might be construed as inappropriate curiosity. No doubt it was some vain concession to fashion.

Their conversation continued in this jesting vein, with an occasional interjection from Mrs. Turner. Miss Turner, I noticed, was not at all interested in fashion or the procurement of notions and baubles. As much as possible, I ignored the voices around me and ate the excellent meal, all the while wondering if perhaps Mr. Winter and his family had retreated into madness after dining at the Turners'.

I was taken by surprise, then, when I heard Mrs. Turner calling my name. "Mr. Vickers? Mr. Vickers?"

"Yes," I said, yanked back to the oppressive reality of the room. "Forgive me. The long journey—"

"Well, of course you must be exhausted!" Mrs. Turner nodded sympathetically. "And Clarissa's nonsense isn't helping one bit. No doubt you'd like to have a few words with Mr. Howard. He farms out in the Big Bottom community, but we're lucky enough to have him visit us whenever he's in town."

I could think of no word to share with the gentleman across the table, but clearly some comment was expected. Casting about for a suitable topic, I finally devised what I thought to be an appropriate opening. "I believe you ride that sorrel horse I saw in town today."

"Red Fox?" Mr. Howard's face lit up with pride. "You saw him, eh? He's the fastest horse in three counties. Yet to lose a race."

"Ah," I said. Having made the acquaintance of an ill-tempered mare in my youth, and having also made an undignified dismount from the back of that she-devil, I had managed quite well on foot and stagecoach ever since. Mr. Howard's enchantment with galloping horses was not a subject I wished to pursue or even to contemplate. "I'm sure you made a clever deal in the purchase," I said to him. One hoped such a comment would be construed by the listener as a compliment, while preserving one from the necessity of untruth.

Either Mr. Howard was as stumped for a topic as I; or he, too, realized that we gentlemen had no common ground upon which to meet, for there was an awkward silence for several seconds.

Recognizing that no further discussion would ensue, Mrs. Turner tried again. "Our Mr. Vickers is the new schoolmaster. All the way from Massachusetts! Won't Jesus Creek be turning out some clever ones?"

"I expect so," agreed Mr. Howard amiably. "I've never been one for books. Other than the Holy Book, of course. My brother is quite the scholar, though. I've often wished to be more like him."

Miss Turner nodded her approval of this worthy ambition.

"Why, Mr. Howard!" declared Miss Clarissa. "Why would a body want to dote on stuffy, musty books? It's a waste of time, if you ask me."

"No one asked you, Clarissa," her mother said with a warning glare.

"Nevertheless, I'd rather live great adventures—or even small ones—than merely read about them." Miss Clarissa tossed her golden head.

I was about to explain the importance of education, which may be useful even to females as they guide their children on the path of higher learning, but Mr. Howard spoke first. "You have an attractive appetite for life, Miss Clarissa," he said.

"You are right, of course, that we should cherish every moment, for the final one comes too soon to everyone. Oh," he turned to me and added, "but of course, book learning can be useful to some."

He did not have to explain who among us most benefits from "book learning." Mr. Howard was a handsome man, obviously well-off and having attained his wealth without benefit of excessive schooling. The world of books and ciphers, as far as he was concerned, existed to provide refuge to those of us less favored by nature.

"You see, Mr. Vickers?" Miss Clarissa said with a gay laugh. "I am a genius."

If the young woman viewed herself so, I would not object. I felt, however, a crushing weight descend upon me along with the realization that, in this harsh frontier world, her sense of priority might be more accurate than my own.

CHAPTER THREE

A WEEK AFTER Dan McClain took physical possession of the Vickers house, the five officers of the Jesus Creek Historical Society arrived on his doorstep, apparently intending to welcome this newcomer to their community with foil-wrapped food and unrelenting friendliness. Not one of them would have admitted that the group was actually involved in a conspiracy.

Sarah Elizabeth Leach, youngest of the conspirators, maneuvered her sturdy old Buick down the rutted driveway and parked it beside the Weaver's Landscaping van. As the Welcome Wagon and Terrorist Society emerged from the car with casserole dishes in hand, they could see the gardening crew and McClain walking off spaces at the back of the house.

"Oh, look!" Delia said to the ladies. "He's torn down the old barn. That probably doubles the value of this place."

"Hmph!" Frankie Mae Weathers, never one to see the bright side of any issue, offered up her warning. "Unless it's just the first step toward tearin' down everything else."

McClain stood out in his tailored jeans and a well-made Aran sweater. Mr. Weaver and the landscapers were dressed more appropriately—in faded denim or coveralls, heavy boots, and ball caps—for the backbreaking task ahead of them.

McClain looked up, then broke away from the intent workers to greet his unexpected company. "Good morning!" he called with a hearty wave of his hand. "How may I help you ladies?"

All of them at once broke into broad smiles and greetings and explanations for their mission, while McClain repeated over and over again, "How nice. How thoughtful. How nice."

Recognizing the dazed expression that Roger so often wore when her friends gathered round him, Delia came to the rescue and coincidentally set her plan in motion. "Why don't we put this food in your refrigerator?" she suggested. "Before it spoils."

"Yes, please. Come in, but I must warn you, the interior looks worse than what you see out here." McClain proved himself a gentleman by taking the covered dishes from Patricia Patrick and Frankie Mae Weathers before leading them inside and pulling out his only bridge chair for elderly Mrs. Lambdin.

He'd been right about the condition of the house. Aside from the dust and stains that Delia had expected, the wallpaper was faded and ripped, and the decades-old floor covering barely showed its pattern through the ground-in dirt. Still, it was far from hopeless; and at a signal from Delia, the Historical Society officers launched into their script.

"Just look at the molding!" Sarah Elizabeth Leach said admiringly, as she ran her fingers around the door frame in the Vickers sitting room. "You don't see that anymore. You're so lucky to live here, Mr. McClain."

The truth was that Sarah Elizabeth knew crackers about molding, but Delia had coached her carefully beforehand: "Everybody admires molding but absolutely nobody wants to get into a protracted conversation about it. Just drop your line on him, be sure he understands that this is valuable molding he's got, and move on."

The others hadn't needed practice, all of them being either history buffs or antique collectors or both. Patricia Patrick had hopped up and down on the linoleum and declared, "Solid oak under there. A little sanding and you'll have the most beautiful floors on earth. They don't make 'em like that anymore."

"I know where you could get the most wonderful slipper chair," Mrs. Lambdin said. "For way less than you'd expect."

Each of the women in attendance managed to find something to contribute to the plot, offering to hand over the names and addresses of companies eager to supply or repair everything needed to return the Vickers house to its original homespun splendor. Delia watched McClain closely and was relieved to see that he appeared to be genuinely interested in what they had to say. With the tiniest of hints from Mrs. Lambdin, he agreed to give them a full tour of the house.

Three upstairs bedrooms may as well have been large trash cans, littered as they were with scraps and bits the auctioneer couldn't force on even the most die-hard bargain hunter. The floors there had never been covered with linoleum, but neither were the solid oak boards in mint condition. It would take years and many, many dollars to bring that part of the house up to snuff. Delia hoped Mr. McClain had a longer attention span and more patience than she.

"Cold up here, isn't it?" Delia wrapped her arms tightly around herself in response to a sudden chill. "I'd advise doubling up on the insulation."

"You've got thin blood," Mrs. Lambdin announced. "You don't eat enough red meat."

Delia let the comment pass; she was used to being warned about the dangers of her vegetarian diet and knew no one listened when she tried to explain the health benefits of soy and grain. True, none of the others seemed to feel the drop in temperature, but maybe they were wearing long johns under their suits.

"I suppose this would have been the master bedroom," Mrs. Lambdin said. "It'll have a pretty view from this window when you've finished your garden."

Delia made a quick visual survey of the room and decided she felt sorry for the "master" who'd slept there. Beneath the fading paint, she could see that there'd once been wallpaper sporting cabbage roses. Gigantic ones. "Can you imagine trying to sleep here?" she asked. "Just look at this wallpaper! It would give me nightmares."

The others looked around, puzzled. "Which wallpaper is that?" McClain asked.

"This wallpaper." Delia reached out and traced a rose with her finger.

"You're startin' to talk like Constance Winter," Frankie Mae snorted. "Whatever paper used to be there is buried under a foot of paint."

Dan McClain subtly herded the ladies out into the hallway. "There are more bedrooms on this floor," he said, "and every one of them in worse shape than this. I suppose I'll get the ground floor in livable condition first, then tackle this part of the house over time."

The stairs, though narrow and steep, were solid enough beneath their feet. McClain took Mrs. Lambdin's arm from behind to steady her descent. The other ladies gripped the banister and followed.

Downstairs, the rooms were a mishmash of centuries and decades. The grand old kitchen at the back of the house was huge, but ruined by cheap floor covering and bare pipes sticking out here and there. Makeshift cabinets had been installed at some point, but the carpenter had been sloppy and the shelves sagged.

Rooms off either side of the kitchen appeared to have been most recently used for storage and bathing, although Delia suspected they'd been bedrooms at one time. The heat from the kitchen woodstove would have helped keep frost off the sleepers' noses during the winter months, but that same heat would have made for unbearable conditions in the summer.

"This bathroom is a dilemma," McClain said, shaking his head. "I love the clawfoot tub, but the rest of the plumbing is hideous."

"This is one time, Mr. McClain," Mrs. Lambdin told him, "when convenience takes precedence over antiquity. Tear out this junk and treat yourself to a whirlpool bath." She ignored Delia's cutting glance. Mrs. Lambdin, after all, was of a generation that had bathed in galvanized tin tubs with water drawn from a well and heated on a woodstove. As far as she was concerned, there was nothing charming about primitive plumbing.

"I'm so glad to know you're all interested in restoring old places like this," McClain told them when he could get a word in edgewise. "Now that I'm retired, I have lots of time on my hands. I'm looking forward to doing the renovation myself."

"Hmph." Frankie Mae Weathers turned away from the window which had held her attention and stared at the newcomer. "I wouldn't think you'd be the type to get your hands dirty."

McClain looked down at his slacks and sweater, then smiled. "I dress like a city boy, don't I?" he admitted. "Actually, I grew up on a farm. Being in business, I've had to project an image. Pretty soon, though, the real me will break through and I'll have paint stains and rips in all my fancy clothes."

"I see you decided not to start just yet." Frankie Mae jerked a finger toward the window. "You got that bunch of snot-nosed landscapers out there."

Weaver and his team moved with perfect synchronization on the spot where the old barn had once stood. Shallow trenches had been made with the back of a shovel to mark off distinct planting areas, and it appeared that an effort was being made to preserve a couple of gnarled old fruit trees. Delia thought it looked like an ambitious garden, but it certainly seemed an odd place to begin restoration. One never knew, though, what an outsider considered a priority.

"Oh, well. I just couldn't wait," McClain explained, as if he'd read her mind. "The barn had to be torn down anyway, and it's almost spring, so I thought, why not start a garden? I wanted at least one pretty, peaceful place to relax while I'm working on the house. I knew it would take me forever to get any kind of yard work done. To tell the truth, I'm not much of a gardener anyway. Barely know a daffodil from a rose."

"Did you ever think of asking your new neighbors for help?" Frankie Mae's nose twitched.

Delia was beginning to catch on. Frankie Mae Weathers, gardener extraordinaire, was miffed at not having been consulted. Fortunately Dan McClain figured it out, too, and rushed to rectify the oversight.

"Would you be willing?" he asked. "I don't want to take up too much of your time, but one thing I've always wanted to do and never had time for was gardening. Flowers, you understand. I planted and hoed enough in my youth that I can grow vegetables without even trying. But flowers—well, I've never had any luck growing them. I guess you have to be born knowing how to do that."

It was the way he'd handled Frankie Mae that concerned Delia. Ever since the ladies had arrived, the impeccably polite Mr. McClain had struck a wrong chord, but Delia hadn't been able to put her finger on the cause.

She'd even chided herself mentally for being uncharitable. After all, the man had allowed his home to be invaded by a group of chattering women. Surely, a successful businessman would have learned along the way how to avoid encounters he didn't enjoy, so McClain must have been slightly pleased to meet them.

He'd greeted them warmly, kept up his end of the conversation, agreed with ideas about Rococo Revival, listened eagerly to suggestions about woven floor covering, and generally fallen in with the plan to save the Vickers homestead. Flawless performance, Delia thought, until he sucked up to Frankie Mae. That had been a little over the top.

And yet, there he was, head inclined as he hung on Frankie Mae's every word about propagation methods. Maybe Delia had been set to dislike him from the start because she'd feared he would tear down the old house and put up a new one, or because Lenny Hemby had said McClain might be a troublemaker. Surely it was possible that Dan McClain was grateful to find himself being accepted into Jesus Creek society so easily.

Another look at him brought an involuntary shake to Delia's head. This wasn't a man who needed acceptance; he had far and away enough self-esteem. And if he'd wanted to get chummy with the neighbors, why had he ignored them all at the auction?

It was more likely that he was cultivating them—the ladies of the Jesus Creek Historical Society—but for what, pray tell? Did he have an overwhelming desire to be elected president of that august organization?

"Tell us, Mr. McClain," Delia said loudly, "how did you happen to pick Jesus Creek? Do you have family around here?" Naturally she already knew that he didn't have family in the town, but that was the only piece of information she'd uncovered so far.

McClain shook his head. "Please call me Dan," he insisted. "I knew I wanted a quiet place to retire. I gave my real estate agent the task of finding what I wanted. She's been on the lookout, and luckily she mentioned this place was going up for auction. The minute I saw the snapshots, I knew I had to have this house. I was tickled to get it at such a good price, too!"

"Oh, so you didn't even inspect the house up close before you bought it?" Delia was surprised that anyone with good sense would shell out hard cash for a pig in a poke. In fact, her intuition told her he wouldn't have done it, that he was lying. But why?

"No need," he said. "From the agent's description and some snapshots, I knew it was perfect. Now tell me, have any of you been involved in major restoration work before? I'd like to hear about your experiences, particularly about the pitfalls. I'm depending on you to save me from making too many mistakes."

The ladies had to admit that none of them had ever undertaken such a monumental task. While some of them lived in homes even older than the Vickers place, those houses had been regularly maintained through the years and the greatest worry the homeowners faced was new roofing every twenty years or so. Delia and Patricia didn't even have historic or particularly interesting homes, just small places suited to single women.

When she could bear the exchange of carpentry information no longer, Delia bluntly changed the subject. "What sort of business were you in before you retired, Mr. McClain?"

"A very dull one," he answered with a laugh. "I can't tell you how happy I am to be out of that world. Jesus Creek is just the haven I need to undo the damage caused by work stress. Tell me about the town. I understand the mayor is quite a character."

For ten minutes or so, Patricia Patrick filled him in on

their mayor's obsession with family values—which had led to the institution of community sing-alongs and Sunday picnics in the park—as well as his predictions of impending UFO infestation. McClain seemed to be enchanted by these tales, unlike most of the locals who found Mayor Mooten tolerable but a tad peculiar.

"Sunday afternoon picnics!" McClain exclaimed. "That sounds wonderful. Do I need an invitation, or may I pop up on my own?"

Patricia, obviously quite taken with the bachelor before her, rushed to assure him that he was more than welcome at the weekly event. "If you feel funny about going alone," she told him, "I'll be glad to pick you up in my car and take you along with me. I could introduce you to everybody."

"That's very kind," McClain said. "Perhaps I could give you a call in a few days and arrange a time. There's some problem about the phone lines, but I expect to have service later this week. And if you haven't heard from me soon," he went on, "please check to be sure the aliens haven't abducted me."

Appreciative laughter was cut short by a determined knock at the front door. Before McClain could cross the room to open it, however, all five of the landscapers had pushed through the door and were fidgeting as if they'd stepped in a nest of seed ticks.

"Mr. McClain," one of the men said, "there's something out here you better see."

"Oh?" McClain said. "What is it?"

"Well, sir, it looks an awful lot like bones. Not dog bones or anything like that, either. I just believe it may be a person."

They were out the door and trotting across the backyard within seconds of the announcement. Even Mrs. Lambdin, who was eighty if she was a day, managed to keep up with the pack.

"Right where we was digging the fish pond," the landscaper explained, still slightly out of breath. "Right there at the back of the lot."

The hole for the pond was not even two feet deep but at

least fifteen feet in diameter. The shallow trench suggested that it would eventually be dug in a figure-eight shape, but for the moment no one was interested in the overall garden plan. There in the perimeter trench lay a clearly identifiable human skull.

"I thought it was a rock at first," the young woman explained. "It was so smooth and pretty. . . . I thought it might be something we could use to edge the pond."

"So you're the one who dug it up?" Delia asked.

The girl nodded. "Yeah. By the time I realized it wasn't a rock, I had it half uncovered. Figured I might as well get it all the way out before I raised the alarm. I put it back in the exact spot where I found it, though. Do you think I'll get in trouble?"

"Kelly here," the landscaper confided as he pointed to the young woman on his crew, "took some sorta college class about finding skeletons."

"Well, not exactly," Kelly demurred. "It came up in a history class. Very often cemeteries are lost under grass or weeds. Especially family plots, because descendants die or move away and no one remembers the graves are there. Markers fall down or they're stolen. There was even a woman in North Carolina who discovered that the stone path by her house was made of headstones someone had stolen from a cemetery! Can you imagine?"

"It's certainly possible that the cemetery was overgrown and forgotten," Delia agreed. "This may have been a family cemetery. There could be several other people buried here, too. I hate to tell you this, Mr. McClain, but you may not get your garden finished in time for spring. Not if there's really a graveyard here."

Delia bent over and examined the specimen without touching it. "It's in bad shape," she called to the startled onlookers. "Several pieces broken loose. I don't know much about bones, but I'm sure you're right, Mr. Weaver. It's human."

Climbing back up to join the others, Delia turned to McClain. "You'd better call the police chief first, and he'll need to bring in an anthropologist. I expect it's been there a while, but if there's even a possibility that this person didn't die of natural causes, the scene will have to be left intact for now."

An ashen-faced McClain nodded dumbly. "I don't have phone lines yet," he reminded her. "And the cell phone doesn't work out here."

"Then we'll take care of it as soon as we get back to town," Delia promised. "Meanwhile, make sure nothing in this yard is touched or disturbed in any way."

She managed to overlook her own potentially damaging behavior, given that she had been extremely careful not to dislodge any portion of the remains. And someone had to investigate, she told herself.

"You think this person was murdered?" young Kelly asked.

"Probably not," Delia assured her. "But it might have some historical importance. We'll call in the authorities and let them sort it out."

The male landscapers and McClain remained fixed in their places, stunned and appalled by the half-exposed skull. Only the girl and the demure ladies of the Jesus Creek Historical Society took death in stride—the first because it was such a foreign concept to her, and the latter because they had come to know it so well.

Mrs. Turner and her elder daughter sat in the darkened parlor, digesting the midday meal. Jeremiah had joined them there, not for companionship, but because heat from the kitchen stove made his small room an oven. He had with him Wilkie Collins's *The Moonstone*, an old favorite which he enjoyed reading again, from time to time.

"Mary, have you read that book?" Mrs. Turner asked of her child. "That one Mr. Vickers has there?"

Mary dutifully looked up from her embroidery and studied the title. "No," she said. "Would you recommend it, Mr. Vickers?"

"She loves to read," Mrs. Turner confided with a meaningful wink. "Always been one for learning. I suppose Mary could have taught school, if she hadn't been needed here at home."

Jeremiah tried to hide his annoyance, but the Turner women truly did gab! "I'm sure you'd be a fine teacher," he said to Mary.

Before Mrs. Turner could further pursue her course, Clarissa bounded down the stairs, skirts hiked well above her ankles. "An amazing thing!" she declared breathlessly. "I was in my room, just resting a bit, when suddenly there came a voice!"

"Clarissa, how many times have I asked you to take the stairs one at a time? Do you listen to anything I ask of you?"

This reprimand reminded Clarissa to brush off her skirt and tuck a loose tress behind her ear but did not diminish her excitement. "But I was in a hurry," she explained. "Don't you want to know what the voice said?"

Mary dropped her head, but her eyes caught Jeremiah's as she spoke. "Young women who hear voices need to be confined for their own safety."

In general, Jeremiah agreed with the diagnosis. He suspected, however, that Clarissa's condition was less severe. "Do you mean to say that, as you dozed, there was a voice in a dream?"

Clarissa waved away the logical explanation for her experience. "Oh no! I wasn't sleeping. I'd only just gotten comfortable. There may have been others, too; I couldn't quite make them out."

Mrs. Turner huffed. "You are making a spectacle of yourself in front of Mr. Vickers," she pointed out. "You'll have him thinking you've lost hold of your senses, crazy as a Winter. Worse still, you'll have him convinced it's a family weakness."

Jeremiah felt his face flush. He most desperately wanted to avoid involvement in this bickering, and he resented the Turner family for holding their disagreements in public. Determining to avoid further awkwardness, he propped *The Moonstone* on his knees and concentrated on the printed words.

"The voice said," Clarissa told them defiantly, "'just look at this wallpaper!' I knew the rose pattern was the best choice. And to think Mary almost talked me out of it."

CHAPTER FOUR

ONE OF THEM OUGHT TO STAY BEHIND until the police chief arrived, Delia decided, in case he needed an eyewitness account. Oh, McClain or the landscapers could serve the purpose, but Delia was sure that a more perceptive observer would be a tremendous help in the matter. Naturally, she elected herself.

"As soon as you get back to town," she'd instructed Sarah Elizabeth and the others, "call Reb and tell him what we've found. I'll wait here with Mr. McClain, just in case. . . ." She couldn't think of any catastrophe that could reasonably require her presence at the scene. "Just in case I'm needed," she added lamely.

Sarah Elizabeth grinned and gave Delia a supportive pat on the back. "Yes, Delia. You stay right here. Guard the crime scene."

"It probably isn't a crime scene," Delia admitted with a trace of disappointment. "Just one lost Indian who ended up here. At most, it's an old cemetery."

"Oh, don't be such a pessimist," Sarah Elizabeth teased her. "I'm sure, if you put your mind to it, you can turn it into a homicide somehow."

"You're too young to be so perceptive," Delia whispered. "Now get these old broads out of here so I can snoop around before the police arrive."

Sarah Elizabeth saluted and bundled the remaining members of the Historical Society into her car. As the Buick drove away down the dirt drive, Dan McClain joined Delia to wave them off.

"Well, so much for my plans to enjoy the water garden," he said.

"You'll have it eventually," Delia consoled him. "After the authorities have done their work. And in the meantime, you've got a mystery to play with. Possibly an entire cemetery in your backyard!"

McClain shook his head. "Surely not. There'd be a record of that, wouldn't there? You can't just misplace a cemetery."

"It happens," Delia said, with the air of one who Knows Such Things. "The thing is, that skull isn't deeply buried. How far down would you say they'd dug before it was exposed?"

McClain took Delia's arm and led her to the backyard where the landscaping crew stood in respectful silence around what would someday be a pond. He studied the scene for a few minutes before saying, "Definitely less than six feet. About two, would you say?"

"If that," Delia suggested. "It can't have been in the ground very long. Not for centuries, I mean. I wonder if it's a Vickers?"

McClain's head snapped around to study her face. "Why would you think that?" he asked.

"This house belonged to the Vickers family for years," Delia explained. "They may have had a small family plot here. As a matter of fact, I bought a trunk full of old papers at the auction, and one of the most valuable items in it turned out to be the memoirs of Jeremiah Vickers. I haven't checked the records, but it seems likely he'd have been the first Vickers to live here. Maybe he built the house."

"That's not the name of the people I bought the house from," McClain reminded her.

Delia nodded. "Yes, well, those were the stepchildren of the last Vickers to live here. The kids and their mother—Dot Orland Hemby Vickers—were in this house for eons. Once Dot passed away, her children inherited. All the same, this house has been called the Vickers house for as long as I can remember."

McClain nodded and chuckled a little. "And will it still be called the Vickers house now that I'm the owner?" he asked.

"Are you kidding? Your new name will be The Fellow Who Lives In The Vickers House. We don't take easily to change in these parts." Delia patted him on the shoulder. "You'll get used to it."

The leader of the landscape team broke ranks to approach McClain and Delia. "You reckon there's any reason for us to hang around?" he asked.

"Reb will want to talk to you, I'm sure," Delia answered. "But you don't have to keep standing here in the yard. Why don't you and your people go sit on the front porch? Have your lunch, if you brought it."

Weaver nodded. "Don't know that any of us want to eat just now, not after that"—he pointed to the skull—"ghoulish thing's been starin' at us, but sittin' sounds like a fine idea." He motioned for his workers to follow him back to the front of the house, away from the scene he found so disturbing, and they escaped in single file. As young Kelly passed, she took one last longing look at the backyard and then winked at Delia. In return, Delia gave the girl a thumbs up, recognizing a kindred spirit.

McClain saw and smiled at Delia. "You and that girl are pretty tough, aren't you?" he commented.

"Why's that?"

"Well, neither of you turned green or squealed. And neither of you seems particularly upset by what we've found. We big brave men will probably have nightmares for a week after this."

"Nonsense," Delia said. "It's bones. Like in a museum. Not the same as finding the actual body of someone we care about." Delia knew from experience that there was a significant difference.

"Of course," McClain said. "I'd forgotten that you were the one. . . ."

"The one?" Delia asked sharply.

"Well, I heard that you'd been involved in a murder a while back. Not involved, that is, but that you'd been the one to find the body." McClain's gaze was steady; he showed no sign of embarrassment about bringing up a sensitive subject.

Delia's earlier misgivings about McClain returned, along with the tiny alarm in her head. How could he know that? It had happened years before and wasn't generally talked about anymore. She couldn't figure out why the man set her nerves on yellow alert. Something was missing, she thought. Some piece of the puzzle was being withheld. And then it occurred to her that, in spite of the best efforts of Jesus Creek's finest busybodies, Dan McClain hadn't revealed one significant fact about himself. "How on earth did you ferret out my life history?" she asked. She forced a small laugh to take the edge off her tone.

"Someone mentioned it," McClain said, without further explanation. "Maybe that explains why you handled today's discovery so well. You've already tackled worse sights than this."

"Yes, that other was much, much worse." Delia still had to fight off the memory from time to time and was doing so at that moment. "I'm surprised you'd have heard about it, though. You haven't been here long. Which local gossip have you been talking to?"

McClain shrugged. "I don't remember. Stories get around here in Jesus Creek, and to tell you the truth, I don't pay much attention. Except when it's something extraordinary, like space aliens or murder."

"Just be sure you take everything with a grain of salt until you've verified it yourself," Delia advised. "We've got some imaginative folks around here."

"And some clever ones." McClain beamed at her. "You've got a reputation for being an excellent researcher. I was hoping you'd help me dig up stories about this house. Who lived here, what became of them all, who first built the house . . . anything like that."

It was, of course, exactly what Delia wanted to hear. "You really do care about preserving this place, don't you? Thank goodness! I was afraid you'd tear it down and build condos."

McClain laughed out loud. "Is *that* why you were all so eager to help me redecorate? You're the historic preservation committee? For a while there, I thought the lot of you owned a construction company and wanted to drum up business."

The tiniest blush colored Delia's face, but she had the

courage to admit the truth. "You're onto us. Onto *me*, I should say. Roger accuses me of trying to move back into the nineteenth century, which is not true at all. I only want to visit there once in a while. But I do want to preserve our history, and I couldn't bear the thought of losing this gorgeous old place to a bulldozer."

"Roger would be the gentleman they refer to as The Crazy Yankee?" McClain asked.

"I haven't heard him called that, but it doesn't surprise me. Roger has a unique way of expressing himself," Delia said tactfully.

"So I've gathered. It's amazing how much I've learned just from having lunch at the diner. The other customers carry on conversations about anything and everything, and they don't care who listens in. Incredible!"

Odd, Delia thought. If he'd been in the diner, Eloise should know as much about the man as his own mother, and it wasn't like her to keep information to herself.

"You aren't used to small towns, I guess," Delia said aloud. "Where did you say you lived before?"

"Oh, I moved around a lot. Nature of the business, you know." Before Delia could pin him down any further, McClain cocked his head to one side and said, "Tell me about those memoirs you found."

"Ah," Delia began. "This Jeremiah Vickers is one longwinded son of a gun. To tell you the truth, I've had trouble staying awake through his pompous scribbling, but after an excruciatingly detailed account of his digestive habits, the poor old guy finally got rolling."

"And what have you learned about him?" McClain asked.

"For one thing," Delia said with relish, "his landlady has him pegged as a husband for her daughter. But Jeremiah Vickers is a mama's boy. He's mentioned her on just about every page so far, and he lives in fear of breaking one of her rules, of which there are many."

Delia had slogged her way through Jeremiah's manuscript, with more than half of it still to go. There was no other way; interspersed among the dry prose and lengthy descriptions of every minute of the most mundane day, she had found valuable nuggets. With all the pointless details Jeremiah had included, Delia couldn't help but wonder what truly fascinating facts he'd left out of his life story.

"He has the most precious throwaway lines," she said. "For instance, my ancestor—also named Delia Cannon, by the way—owned the town's first tavern."

McClain kept a straight face as he asked, "Does this raise or lower your position in the community?"

"Frankly? I'd be better off socially if she'd been some Confederate general's concubine." Delia, though she shared the town's obsession with history, did not take it personally. "Anyway," she went on, "Jeremiah had his first encounter with Delia, the saloon owner, just shortly after he got to town. Imagine his surprise when he rolled into church and found out *she* was the song leader!"

Delia had laughed until her sides ached when she'd read Jeremiah's description of the experience. "He decided on the spot that it wasn't really a church at all, but a gathering of heathens out to capture his soul."

McClain proved himself a good audience by laughing with her. "Did he hop the first freight train back to Mother?" he asked.

"He never even told her! He was afraid the shock of it would kill Mumsie where she stood, so he 'concluded to omit that part of the narrative.'"

"And did he ever go to church again?" McClain asked. "Or did he cower in his room on Sundays?"

"Fortunately, another boarder at Mrs. Turner's Halfway House was able to talk sense into him." Delia knew McClain was only being polite and that she should stop before his face took on that strained smile she'd seen so often on Roger. On the other hand, she'd been eager to share her discovery, and Mr. McClain *had* started this conversation, hadn't he?

"So Jeremiah Vickers lived in this very house?" McClain asked.

"I don't know," Delia admitted, "but it's a reasonable assumption. Would you like me to check into it? There's bound to be a record. I've never had any reason to trace the Vickers family, but if you're interested—"

"Absolutely!" McClain assured her with sincere enthusiasm. "I want to know more about Jeremiah, for one thing. And about his children and his adventures on the wild frontier. Did he marry the landlady's daughter? Did he return home to dear old mom?"

Delia's stomach fluttered. It seemed that her wish was coming true: McClain was restoring the house and he was interested in the history of its previous occupants.

"You know," she said, "with that attitude, you could end up being president of the Historical Society. Provided you're willing to kill a few of the more determined candidates."

Suppertime in the Turner household had quickly become a dreaded event for Jeremiah. Oh, the food was tasty and plentiful, but swallowing it was made nearly impossible by Mrs. Turner's insistence on conversation.

"Mary, dear," she would say, several times during the meal, "have more of this bread. You eat like a bird. Doesn't she eat like a bird, Mr. Vickers?"

What was Jeremiah to say? In his opinion, Miss Mary Turner's eating habits were her own affair. She seemed healthy enough, although given to swooning at regular intervals. His mother also swooned whenever she was upset, but otherwise her physical condition was sound.

"Maybe if she got out more," Clarissa said. "Took some exercise. It would benefit her appetite."

If Clarissa were an example, this would be good advice. That young woman walked back and forth to town on any day she could escape her mother's watchful eye; she had been known to swim in the nearby creek when the mood struck her; and on one occasion, Jeremiah had glimpsed her astride the workhorse, her skirt tucked in and exposing her stockings for all the world to see.

Unlike her sister, Clarissa was always ravenous and ate her meals with gusto, even when she'd just an hour before snitched a piece of pie or a drumstick from the kitchen. And yet, Jeremiah noted, she maintained a handsome figure.

J. D. Howard was no more eager than Jeremiah to give an opinion of the subject at hand, and so he endeavored to steer conversation to another topic. "I've heard talk," he said, "of putting a statue in the town. To honor veterans of the recent war."

"Oh, they talk," Mrs. Turner fussed. "It'll not get done in our lifetime."

"Best not to dwell on the past, anyway," Mary said. "It only brings up memories of pain and loss."

Howard made no response, but his head nodded gently.

"If the town is putting anything to the vote," Clarissa chimed in, "I'd rather it be for a change of name. Division Street. Ugh. It's ugly to say. I'd prefer to call it something pretty, maybe give it a flower name. *Primrose.* Or *Morning Glory.*"

"Clarissa, do you never think of weighty matters?" Mary asked. She made no attempt to hide the derogatory nature of her question.

"I have agreed," Howard said, loud enough to interrupt the bickering, "to preach the sermon this Sunday. Brother Bagwell has been called across the river to attend a family matter. I'm thinking of using the lesson of the walls of Jericho, to remind one and all that perseverance is stronger than the greatest obstacle." He cast a brief glance at the Turner sisters, then said with a smile, "Or perhaps I'll dwell on the story of Cain and Abel, as a warning against sibling disharmony."

CHAPTER FIVE

DELIA RECOGNIZED the ancient muffler of Police Chief Reb Gassler's pickup truck and led McClain back to the front yard.

"There's only one patrol car," she explained when she saw McClain's reaction to Reb's truck. "It's in the shop. We actually have a very fine mounted police force here, but Reb can't seem to get the hang of riding horses—truthfully, he's just too stubborn to give it a chance—so he uses his personal transportation instead."

"Curiouser and curiouser," McClain said from the side of his mouth. Stepping forward, he met Reb as the police chief stepped out of his pickup. "Chief, I'm Dan McClain. I own this place."

Reb looked McClain over carefully, then looked past him to Delia for confirmation. "Dee?"

Delia nodded, and Reb held out his hand to McClain.

"You took long enough getting here, Reb. It's been over half an hour since the ladies left here to call you," Delia chided. "I'm sorry if we pulled you away from a good lunch."

Reb nodded. "I was halfway through a fine roast beef plate, complete with mashed potatoes and Eloise's biscuits, but this sounded too good to miss. Sarah Elizabeth says there's a skeleton in the backyard. Mrs. Lambdin swears she saw it move. Patricia Patrick says it's the remains of a war hero murdered by some worthless Yankee renegade. Frankie Mae says it's D. B. Cooper. Y'all got any other information to add?" he asked, straight-faced.

"Its grandmother was a Cherokee princess," Delia said, straight-faced.

Both men stared at her.

"Genealogical humor," she explained. "Everybody in the South claims to have a Cherokee princess in the family. Nobody really does."

Reb and McClain found this less than fascinating and moved the conversation along to the matter at hand. "Who are all those people on the porch?" Reb asked.

"My landscapers," McClain told him. "They're the ones who actually found the skull. They were digging a small pond out back when they came across it."

"I'll have a chat with 'em, then," Reb said and ambled across the yard to take statements from the witnesses. "Y'all may as well join me," he added. "Looks cooler over here in the shade."

Delia trotted after him, with McClain bringing up the rear. Reb's concession to the modern world was a small tape recorder for note-taking, which he pulled out of his shirt pocket. It was, he reluctantly admitted, easier and more reliable than handwritten notes, although he remained suspicious of all gadgets and gizmos which operated with more than one moving part.

The landscapers told their tale, which took little time since their day had been perfectly ordinary until they had made the gruesome discovery. "So that's all? You didn't find anything beforehand that would've led you to expect this?" Reb concluded.

"No, sir," Weaver said passionately. "If I'd have thought it'd come to this, I'd have never started the job. I don't need dead bodies turning up in my work."

"It's not exactly a body," Delia reminded him. "Just a skull."

"All the same. . . ," Weaver said.

"We'll have to find out if the rest of it's here," Reb said. "Which means calling in the state people. Mr. McClain, I'm gonna have to rope off your yard. Mr. Weaver, whatever equipment you've got back there will just have to stay until the higher-ups say you can take it away. Sorry 'bout that."

Weaver was not happy about it, but he was also disinclined to engage in battle with the forces of law and order.

"Just hurry 'em up, will ya?" he pleaded. "I've got a living to make."

"I'll do what I can," Reb said sympathetically. "You may as well go on. Still time to get in some fishing this afternoon."

The landscapers left without argument, although Kelly looked as if she'd have been glad to stay behind and monitor the rest of the investigation. Delia was becoming quite fond of that girl.

With the crowd out of his way, Reb turned full attention to Dan McClain. "So you're the fella who bought the Vickers place," he pronounced.

McClain glanced at Delia, acknowledging her powers of prophecy. "Yes," he said. "I've been here about a week now. Nice town."

Reb's eyebrows shot up immediately. "You like it here? Where you from?"

"Of course I like it here!" McClain exclaimed. "I'm looking forward to getting to know everyone and to becoming a part of the community. I suppose I'll be the talk of the town after this, won't I?"

"Uh-huh," Reb agreed. "Now you hired Mr. Weaver and his people to come out and dig a hole in your yard. You want to put a pond back there, is that right? Back where the barn used to be?"

"A small pond. A garden pool, really."

"Let's have a look, then," Reb said and stepped carefully off the sagging porch.

Delia and McClain accompanied him around the house, where the shallow pit gaped open in the middle of the yard. "You can just peek from back here," Delia pointed out. "Try not to leave footprints in the loose soil. You know the state investigator won't like that."

"She can get over it," Reb growled.

The area was cluttered with Weaver's equipment, but at least it had been cleared of the thatch and debris which littered the rest of the yard. With the old barn gone, Delia could see that McClain would have a clear view of the surrounding woods. The trees would be breathtaking in most seasons;

for the moment, though, they stood like stark sentinels around the perimeter of the Vickers property.

"It really will be a lovely garden," Delia noted. "Eventually. I wonder if any of those fruit trees can be saved." A small orchard of pear and apple trees struggled to survive, in spite of long neglect.

"If not, I'll replant," McClain told her.

Reb looked into the pit just long enough to assure himself that a skull really existed there, then turned back to the other two. "Okay, that's enough for me. I don't know nothing about old bones, but I'm pretty sure this one's way past the point of my jurisdiction. Time to call the big boys. Mr. McClain, you might want to get yourself a hotel room until they finish excavating. Shouldn't take more'n a day or two."

"Oh, I'm sure they won't bother me," McClain replied. "And I'll make it a point to stay out of their way. I want this wrapped up as quickly as possible," he said, then added, "so that I can get on with my restoration."

"Don't blame you," Reb agreed. "They'll want to talk to Lenny and Lodina, of course. Dee, remind me to stop by Lenny's on the way back to town. And I expect they'll have a lot of questions for you, too, Mr. McClain. Most likely you won't know the answers, since you just moved in here and all. Unless you knew the Vickers family before?"

"It seems to me that Delia is the one they should talk to," McClain offered. "She's the historian. In fact, she was just telling me about a diary."

"*The Memoirs of Jeremiah Vickers*," Delia explained. "It was in that trunk I bought at the estate auction. I'm not sure yet just how Jeremiah fits into the family—he first came to Jesus Creek around 1878—but I'll keep you posted as I learn."

"I'd appreciate that," McClain said enthusiastically. "Obviously I've bought a house with a history. Who knows what evil deeds old Jeremiah committed?" McClain playfully arched a brow.

Reb nodded toward the grave of their unidentified skull. "I'd appreciate it if that fellow in your yard turns out to be Jeremiah's victim, then. Or it can be Jeremiah himself, for that matter. Just so long as whoever it is died a long, long time ago and I don't get stuck with the paperwork."

This sent a tremor of excitement through Delia, who was suddenly itching to leave the scene of the mystery and get home to any clues she could find in the memoirs of a man who might have been a killer.

"You notice anything odd about him?" Reb spoke quietly even though McClain had gone inside to prepare cold drinks for the three of them.

"In what way?" Delia asked innocently. She was glad, actually, that Reb had brought it up. If he was curious about McClain it meant she wasn't letting her imagination run away with her. Or maybe they were both suspicious of outsiders in general. Jesus Creekians tended toward paranoia.

"He doesn't answer questions," Reb said. "Not that I object to people keeping to themselves, mind. It's a refreshing change. All this touchy-feely sharing-my-emotions gets on my nerves. But—"

"But he doesn't even answer when you ask where he's from," Delia finished. "I noticed, yes."

"What do you know about him?" There was no doubt in Reb's mind that Delia knew something.

With a quick glance at the house to assure herself that McClain was still inside, Delia dropped her voice and said, "He has no family here that I can find. No connections to Jesus Creek at all, for that matter. He found out about the auction through the local real estate company, contacted them by phone. He'd been looking for a place here for over a year, but nothing struck his fancy until the Vickers place went up for auction. Andie Summers was the agent who put him onto it, and she says he paid full price with a check drawn on a San Francisco bank."

Reb waited, but Delia said no more. "That's it? That's all you've found out about him?"

"What do you expect, miracles? I'm not a private investigator, and in any case, there's no reason to snoop around in Mr. McClain's life. He hasn't done anything wrong or even—"

"Has that ever stopped you before?" Reb asked. "He's up to something, for sure. If he's got enough money to pay cash for this property, and if he's from the big city, then what caused him to settle in Jesus Creek?"

Delia shook her head. "He says he wants a quiet, peaceful retirement." They rolled their eyes at each other before Delia went on. "Maybe he wanted to be isolated because he's starting a cult. Boy, is he in for a surprise when he finds out who his competition is!"

She was referring to the local group known as the Brotherhood of Strength, which, while not proven to be a cult or anything else more serious than a good-old-boys' club, had Delia and several other residents on their toes. Reb's young officer, Kay Martin, had made exposing the truth about the Brotherhood of Strength a personal goal, but so far she'd found nothing against them which would hold up in court.

"He might be planning to open a casino out here," Reb mused. "Any local talent that could double as lounge singers?"

"That's stretching a bit," Delia replied. "If he wanted to open a casino, he'd have gone on to Mississippi, don't you think?"

"I suppose we could ask him outright what his intentions are," Reb suggested. "Reckon he'd answer the question?"

At that moment the screen door slammed and Dan McClain stepped off his back porch, carefully avoiding the rotted-through top step. "Ice water all around," he announced cheerfully.

"Just the thing," Reb said, accepting a jelly-jar glass. "You've got well water out here, haven't you? Lucky dog."

McClain sipped from his own glass and smiled. "Amazing how good pure water is. Nothing like it."

"I don't guess you get anything like this"—Reb held up his glass—"back where you're from."

"Surely can't," McClain agreed. He gazed off into the distance, savoring the view of the wooded hills which surrounded his property. "I've dreamed about being here, and it's finally real."

"Oh?" Delia asked. "Jesus Creek must have made quite an impression on you. When were you here before?"

McClain blinked and turned his full attention to her. "I've been here a lot in my mind," he said and grinned sheepishly. "Some of us just aren't cut out for the fast lane. No matter where I've gone or what I've done, I've always wanted to be on my own piece of land, swinging on the front porch, maybe even feeding some chickens. I'll bet I could put the coop right over there." He pointed to a far corner of the yard.

"You might be disappointed," Reb reminded him. "Small towns are pretty dull. We don't have much in the way of entertainment here."

"I've been here less than a week. Delia and her friends have come to visit, brought me food, and offered an assortment of favors. The mayor fears an invasion by Klingons. This morning, I found a body in my backyard. What do you call excitement, Chief?"

There was no schoolhouse in Jesus Creek, of course. Until Jeremiah's arrival, education had depended upon parents and the late Mrs. Bretharte, who had taught reading and penmanship in her modest home until her death.

The town's only church had been donated for use as a school during the week. Classes would not begin until September, and it was now only mid-August, but Jeremiah was eager to assess the arrangement. There was also a need for one or two personal items, and so he headed into town on foot.

"Oh, dear!" Mrs. Turner exclaimed when she heard his plan. "I do wish you'd mentioned it sooner. The girls have just left in the wagon, or you could have ridden into town with them. But you'll surely meet up with them there and have a convenient way home."

As he walked, Jeremiah considered the easy way Mrs. Turner referred to her establishment as "home." Naturally she thought of it as such, but Jeremiah could have pointed out that his home was far distant. No doubt Mrs. Turner's motherly disposition caused her to consider all her boarders as little chicks. Jeremiah wouldn't dream to dispossess her of her delusion, but any reasonably perceptive mind could quickly deduce that Jesus Creek would never be home to him.

There was a rustic charm to the area, of course, despite the hot and dusty conditions of late summer. Trees lined the path between the boardinghouse and town. A few wildflowers still survived the drought, adding cheer to the countryside. And birds of every variety chattered the news of his passage.

All in all, Jeremiah's peaceful excursion into Jesus Creek was an enjoyable outing. Until he reached his destination, that is. He was horrified by the sight of Clarissa standing just feet away from the tavern door, engaged in animated conversation with Elmer Winter. Mrs. Turner, as well as his own mother, would expect Jeremiah to rush to the aid of the lady. "Miss Clarissa!" he called in greeting. "Perhaps it would be best if you stepped across the street with me, away from—"

"Oh, good morning, Mr. Vickers." Clarissa had dressed suitably for the weather, in a pale blue linen frock. Still, her face glowed in the heat, and damp tendrils escaped her dainty bonnet. "You know Mr. Winter, of course."

The town drunkard touched a hand to his forehead, smirked in greeting, then drank from the bottle he carried close to his chest.

"We were just talking about you," Clarissa went on. "Mr. Winter says the Steiner boys are roaming today. You'll not enjoy having them in your schoolroom. They're wild as lions."

"A small amount of discipline," Jeremiah explained, "effects enormous change."

Elmer Winter coughed and spat.

Ignoring this, Jeremiah returned to his original purpose— to rescue Mrs. Turner's daughter from an embarrassing situation. "I find myself in need of some small items. Will you accompany me to Mooten's store?" he encouraged.

"Why, yes!" Clarissa agreed, to Jeremiah's relief. "I was heading there when I met up with Mr. Winter. If you'll excuse us, sir?"

Without a word, Winter shambled back into the saloon, nearly colliding with another of his kind as they passed in the doorway.

Even though it was midweek, the town buzzed with activity. Several horses and wagons stood along the street's edge, as their owners bustled about from store to bank to stable. Jeremiah noted with distaste that most of the traffic was centered around Delia's Tavern.

"Mr. Winter says the weather is unnatural," Clarissa told him as they crossed the main street. "He says there's a storm brewing."

"I don't believe a late summer storm is unnatural," Jeremiah replied.

"Oh, he doesn't mean a rain storm," Clarissa explained. "Mr. Winter sees beyond the ordinary world. He says this is a spiritual storm that will blow away illusion and rain down misery."

Jeremiah scoffed at such nonsense, of course. "Miss Clarissa," he said, "you mustn't give heed to a madman's words."

"I know it sounds incredible." She paused as a small farm wagon passed in front of them. "But Mr. Winter is no charlatan who converses with the spirits in darkened rooms."

"No," Jeremiah agreed. "Mr. Winter is a lost soul whose mind is clouded by the demons in that bottle he cherishes."

"There's no denying he has the unfortunate habit," Clarissa conceded. "But haven't we all made unwise decisions at one time or another?"

Jeremiah took her elbow to assist her in the step up to the boarded walk. "Education teaches us how to avoid most poor choices," he pointed out, harking back to his earlier argument. "Those books you find useless contain warnings, if we read carefully and engage our wits."

For some reason this made Clarissa laugh. "Then there's the kind of wit employed by Mr. Winter. In his way, he's an innocent. His eyes see what we ordinary mortals ignore because we've been taught to ignore it."

"More likely," Jeremiah explained, "his eyes see what isn't there at all."

"Mr. Vickers, you ought to consider all the possibilities in heaven and on earth. Mr. Winter is a force we can't understand, but his warnings benefit us all."

"He fails to recognize the danger that awaits him in that establishment. I doubt he can steer the rest of us away from peril." As soon as he'd said it, Jeremiah felt a sharp pain in the middle of his back. "Oh!" he cried, then immediately heard peals of laughter. Turning, he saw that three boys large enough to be pulling plows were entertaining themselves at his expense. Two of them held pebbles, poised for throwing.

The third was empty-handed, having just released his projectile which hit Jeremiah squarely in the shoulder. "Don't turn your back, Teacher!' the boy taunted. "If they make us get schoolin', we'll teach you how it works."

"Boys," Jeremiah said evenly, "this is no behavior for gentlemen. You'll learn in time—"

The three hooligans closed in upon Jeremiah and Clarissa, their wicked grins now turned to threatening glares. Jeremiah backed away as the ringleader poked a grimy finger in his chest. "You'll be sorry if you cross us," the boy warned.

Such blatant disrespect for authority left Jeremiah speechless and, he realized, terrified. If these were to be his students—

"Richie Steiner!" Clarissa's tiny hand flew out and soundly smacked the boy's cheek. "I'll have no trouble from you or your brothers." She slapped him again for good measure. "Go wipe your chin, and don't let me hear of you bothering Mr. Vickers again, or I'll be sure to tell it to your father."

The rage in Clarissa's voice, along with her violent assault on the boys, persuaded the three to remove themselves from that location. Nevertheless, their faces did not assure Jeremiah that a lesson had been learned.

"Never mind them," Clarissa said soothingly. "The whole family is spoiled as month-old milk."

It wasn't the boys that Jeremiah minded, but the audience of amused onlookers, including Elmer Winter, who snickered at his red face. No doubt word would spread quickly— the new schoolmaster had been rescued from ruffians by a slip of a girl.

CHAPTER SIX

DELIA CLUNG TO THE SEAT of Reb's pickup as they bounced along the winding back road into town. "Do you have shock absorbers?" she finally snapped.

"What for?" Reb asked. "You're getting too soft, living with all those high-tech conveniences like air-conditioning and running water. You ought to take lessons from your new neighbor back there."

"McClain has running water," she reminded him. "And electricity. Five minutes into a Tennessee summer, and I guarantee he'll have air-conditioning, too. His ideas about getting back to the land will vanish in a week. Two at the most, and he'll go running back to civilization. You know how these would-be country boys are."

McClain had invited Delia to return the next day, when, Reb estimated, the state investigator and her team would arrive to complete the excavation. "I wouldn't miss it!" she'd assured him. "I freely admit to being too curious for my own good."

Delia was not the romantic one might have assumed, though. She knew the skull in McClain's backyard was most likely left over from some nomadic tribe which had passed through the area centuries before and never returned. At best, the archeologists would find a Clovis point buried with it.

True, it hadn't been buried deeply, but that meant nothing for the time being. Maybe, years ago, a plow had churned up the soil. And, too, the skull had been protected by the Vickers's barn for who knew how long.

There was the slim but tantalizing possibility that Jeremiah Vickers had been the Sawny Bean of his time. Delia hoped, if that proved to be the case, that Jeremiah hadn't left any descendants behind to carry the gene.

There wasn't a single Vickers in her family tree. That in itself struck her as odd; Jesus Creek was a small place, and most of the current inhabitants were the tail end of families who had settled in the area almost two centuries before. With only one Vickers family accounted for, it was a safe bet that Jeremiah had been the patriarch, and now his line had died out in the area.

Instead of driving straight into town and dropping Delia off at her own house, Reb had chosen to stop by Lenny's first, to warn him that the state investigators would be coming along to ask questions. "Maybe I'll catch Lodina at her brother's," he said. "If not, I'll walk over to her place after I get you home. How do you think they'll react to this? Finding bones on their property, I mean."

"Well, it's not their property anymore," Delia reminded him. "So maybe they won't care at all."

She tried to put herself in the place of Lenny and Lodina, but there was nothing in her life history with which to compare such a surprise. The bones didn't belong to a Hemby, so it didn't concern the Hemby heirs. Neither Lenny nor Lodina took an interest in history or genealogy, so they weren't likely to care about some long-dead stranger buried in a yard that no longer belonged to them anyway.

Was there a Vickers descendant somewhere who would care?

"What?" Reb asked.

"Just thinking about families. In particular about the Vickers family. Is that Kay?" Delia pointed to a woman in the street ahead of them.

"Gotta be," Reb said, slowing the truck. "You know anybody else who'd jump up and down and flap her arms like a crazed turkey?" He brought the pickup to a stop directly in front of Lenny Hemby's tree-shaded house. Kay was beside them instantly, talking a blue streak before Reb could roll down his window.

"You're supposed to have your beeper with you all the

time, Reb!" she reminded him sharply.

Apparently Kay had gotten beeped instead, and Delia could see why the girl was short-tempered. Dressed in turquoise sweat pants and a red plaid shirt, Kay stood there barefoot. If she didn't catch her death of cold from that, roaming about in the February temperatures with wet hair hanging down her back would surely do the job.

"I've got the danged thing right here." Reb patted his shirt pocket to prove his innocence.

"Reb." Kay reached through the window and yanked the beeper from his shirt. "You're supposed to have it turned on."

"If it's turned on, they'll beep me," Reb said reasonably.

"How many times—forget it. Listen, we've got a big problem here. Lenny Hemby is upstairs in his bed, dead as a dodo, and it is not from natural causes."

For the first time, Reb and Delia looked closely at the house beside them. Lodina sat on the top step, arms wrapped around her knees, staring into the distance. Beside her, Lenny's next-door neighbor, Patricia Patrick, kept patting Lodina's back. Delia could see Patricia's lips move, but there was no response from Lodina.

"Have you called the coroner?" Reb asked.

"Here he comes now." Kay indicated the Jeep Cherokee coming toward them. "Why don't you pull your junker off the road, Reb?"

Kay jogged away to meet Dr. James, the Jesus Creek family physician who doubled as the county coroner, while Reb pulled his pickup into Lenny's paved driveway behind Lodina's little Toyota.

"Looks like you'll have to walk from here," he said to Delia. "Sorry about that, Dee."

"Don't worry about it. I've been getting home by myself for years," she reminded him. "I don't have to point out that you've got more important chores to tend to." She opened the passenger door and lowered herself to the ground. "You don't have a pair of shoes in the truck, do you? For Kay?"

"Sorry," Reb said. "I try to be prepared for anything, but it never once occurred to me to pack size 6 Mary Janes."

Delia and Reb proceeded side by side up the cracked concrete walk to Lenny's front porch. Under his breath, Reb muttered, "You are not going inside that house, Dee."

"Only far enough to comfort Lodina," she whispered back. "You think I want to see what's in there?"

As they approached the porch, Patricia looked up with a pleading glance. "I can't get her to leave," she said helplessly.

Lodina sat on the top step, her body folded in half so that her head almost dropped below her knees. She'd wrapped her arms around herself, and even though she was dressed in wool slacks and a jacket, she shivered uncontrollably. If she cried, she did it silently.

Reb squatted in front of the two women and looked directly into Lodina's unfocused eyes. "Lodina, you need to go home with Patricia. Go on, now. I'll come over there in a while and talk to you."

Like a zombie, Lodina rose and took a shaky step to the ground. Patricia and Delia instantly assumed caretaker positions on either side of her, steering her gently across the yard and away from the crime scene. As they guided Lodina toward Patricia's house next door, Delia glanced over her shoulder and reminded Reb: "Shoes for Kay."

They settled an unresistant Lodina in Patricia's guest bedroom, made sure she was tucked and bundled under blankets and comforters, then retreated to the kitchen to wait for Reb. For the moment, there was nothing else they could do to be useful.

"Do you have any idea what happened?" Delia asked. She'd seated herself at the counter while Patricia made coffee and sliced freshly baked brownies that neither of them would eat.

"Not one," Patricia said. Once the brownies were piled on a serving plate, she ran water in the sink and began scrubbing the pan. "Sarah Elizabeth dropped me off first after we got back to town. I came right in and made these brownies for my book discussion group tonight. We're reading that one you recommended, Delia—that new one by Teri Holbrook—and you're exactly right. It's a wonderful book! I couldn't put it down!"

Pleased as she was that the book group enjoyed one of her favorite authors, Delia preferred to remain on the subject of Lenny. "How did you find out that . . . that there was a problem?"

Patricia dried the clean pan and shook the dish towel briskly before hanging it on a hook beneath the sink. Then she poured two cups of coffee, produced spoons, sugar sub-stitute, and powdered fat-free creamer, and handed Delia an embroidered napkin. Patricia's nervous energy was legendary, and for the moment it threatened to set off avalanches in the Alps.

"I'd just taken the brownies out of the oven," she said finally, "when I went out to get the mail. I didn't even notice at first, not until I had my hand in the mailbox. I just looked up and there was Lodina, standing out in front of Lenny's place. Standing like a statue, I mean, not moving a muscle."

Delia tried to hurry the story along. "So you went over there. . . ."

Patricia nodded, her head bobbing up and down like it was on a spring. "I could tell something was wrong, so I went run-ning over. And Delia, she didn't even look at me, but when I got up to her, she said, 'Lenny's dead. Call somebody.'"

"Lodina found him . . . like that?" Delia asked. It was a horrifying thought.

Patricia's eyes filled with tears. "She was over there every day, usually to fix a meal for Lenny. They took care of each other that way, you know. She'd cook for him and do his grocery shopping. Lenny kept up her yard and her car and all."

Delia couldn't imagine what it had been like for Lodina, finding her brother dead in his own home. She didn't *want* to imagine it, either. "Do you think," she asked Patricia, "that Lodina understood what had happened? That he'd been killed, I mean. Or does she think he died naturally?"

Delia's concern was for Reb. She'd hate for him to have to break the news to Lodina. She looked up to find Patricia star-ing at her.

"Oh, my goodness!" Patricia wiped at her eyes with her napkin. "Oh, Delia. I had no idea. I just took it for granted he'd had a heart attack!"

Of course! Delia thought. Patricia knew no more than what Lodina had told her—that Lenny was dead. Kay would have been careful to keep quiet about the details, and Delia knew the cause of death only because she'd been with the police chief when Kay reported to him.

"I'm an idiot," she said. "Patricia, I'm sorry I blurted it out."

"That's okay," Patricia told her. "Don't you worry about it. You're probably in shock, too. Of course, you don't know what you're saying."

In shock? Delia considered the possibility of this. She certainly was stunned and confused, but in recent years she'd found very little actually shocked her. "You know," she said, more to herself than to Patricia, "when we find out the reason for Lenny's death, we'll all be shocked. It never fails, does it? The motive for any murder is always totally ludicrous."

In due time, Reb and Dr. Daryl James arrived at Patricia's. "Thought I'd better check on Lodina," Dr. James said.

Patricia led him down the hall to the guest room, leaving Reb to fend off Delia's questions.

"I didn't expect to find you still here," he said.

Delia glanced at her watch. "Good grief! I had no idea I'd been here this long. But never mind that—what have you learned about Lenny's death?"

"Far as we can tell, they didn't take a thing," he said. He pulled Delia to the door and kept his voice low, lest Lodina hear any of the remarks. "No break-in, no theft, no vandalism. Looks like somebody just caught him asleep in bed and shot him right through the heart with one of his own guns."

Delia could only sigh at the senseless nature of the crime. So far, no one had invented the words to express the amount of anger such an act summoned up.

"I know," Reb said. "Cold-blooded. Downright evil, in my opinion. It'll be even worse when we make an arrest. I don't want to believe it of any of us."

"You don't think"—Delia glanced at the hallway to be sure no one was coming—"that Lenny might have. . . ?"

"Not a chance," Reb assured her. "Not unless the gun got up and walked off by itself. I've dug into every crevice in that house, and there's no murder weapon."

"But no break-in?" Delia asked.

"No need," Reb told her. There was a trace of anger in his voice. "Lenny didn't have a single door or window locked. Some people just don't get it. The world is not a friendly place."

He didn't have to convince Delia; she even locked her car doors when driving around Jesus Creek. She reasoned that every town has a first carjacking, and she didn't intend to hold that title.

The trouble was, people like Lenny Hemby were great believers in the basic goodness of other human beings. Sadly, they were often victims of their own faith, and in cases like this one, they'd never have a chance to rethink the doctrine.

The Jesus Creek Public Library boasted an impressive genealogy and local history section, thanks to Delia and the Historical Society. Unfortunately, Delia couldn't get to it until she'd updated Sarah Elizabeth Leach, the librarian, on everything that had happened since the ladies left McClain's.

Pulling Sarah Elizabeth into the small office, Delia closed the door firmly behind her. "Bad news," she said.

"Oh, no!" Sarah Elizabeth's wide eyes grew to the size of demitasse cups. "Don't tell me it's already been identified. I thought that would take days. Is it someone we know? Did Reb arrest that McClain man?"

Delia held up both hands to stop Sarah Elizabeth. "It isn't the skull. I'm talking about *really* bad news."

The younger woman's face went instantly white, her body stiffened as if in preparation for a physical blow and her voice tightened around the words. "What is it? Is it Ariel?"

"No, no, no!" Delia should have known better than to say "bad news" to a young mother before assuring Sarah Elizabeth that her child was fine. "Ariel's okay. It's not her."

Sarah Elizabeth's relief was so great that she nearly collapsed as her body relaxed. Since the worst thing imaginable had not happened, she was ready for whatever Delia threw at her.

"Lenny Hemby is dead," Delia explained. "Someone shot him."

"What? Why?" No longer terrified, Sarah Elizabeth shifted to stunned amazement. "Does Reb know?"

Delia nodded. "He was driving me back to town when we found out. All I know so far is that someone shot Lenny in his sleep. Lodina found him. She's okay, but mostly because she's in shock."

"But I still don't understand," Sarah Elizabeth said. "Was it a robbery? Did Lenny put up a fight?"

"No," Delia said. "Reb told me the doors weren't locked, so a robber could've walked off with anything. But nothing was stolen. It looks like someone went there specifically to kill Lenny."

"That sweet old man," Sarah Elizabeth sighed. "Who would do that? And why? I mean, old as he was, Lenny would've died on his own pretty soon."

Delia, herself old enough to be Sarah Elizabeth's mother, hadn't thought of it, but that was a peculiar thing. "Ordinarily," she said, "I'd wonder who inherits. In this case, though, it's bound to be Lodina, and she certainly isn't a suspect."

"Oh, dear," Sarah Elizabeth said. "She'll be lost without Lenny. They've been like best friends ever since—" She stopped, letting her mouth fall open.

Most people in Jesus Creek saw Sarah Elizabeth as a bouncy, chatty, harmless young girl. It didn't matter that she'd taken on the responsibility of motherhood with a vengeance, cared for her elderly mother-in-law, maintained the family home, and held down a full-time job. Less perceptive souls would have dismissed the sudden gleam in Sarah Elizabeth's eyes, but Delia had found her to be perceptive beyond her years. She was inclined to believe that whatever had just occurred to Sarah Elizabeth was worth hearing. "Ever since what?" she asked.

Sarah Elizabeth dropped her voice a notch, as if she were about to commit blasphemy. "What if Lodina doesn't inherit from Lenny? What if his ex-wife gets everything?"

Delia wanted to believe she'd have thought of it herself in time, but she gave credit where it was due. "You should be working for Reb," she said as praise. "How long has it been since the divorce?"

"Beats me," Sarah Elizabeth said. "I wasn't here when it happened."

Delia figured it in her head. "At least ten years, and I don't know whether Lenny had anything to do with her after the divorce."

"She moved away?" Sarah Elizabeth asked.

"Oh, yes. Caroline never did fit in here. Their marriage might have gone better if Lenny had packed up and moved to . . . wherever she came from. I don't remember."

"Was it a nasty divorce?" Sarah Elizabeth asked. "Or a chummy one?"

Delia thought about her answer before she spoke. "I've never heard Lenny say a word against Caroline, but Lodina never liked her."

"Well, it's something to look into," Sarah Elizabeth concluded. "I'll mention it to Reb. You know, whoever does inherit from Lenny has a better deal now that the Vickers place has been sold."

Another point that would have occurred to Delia shortly. "Lenny told me he was worried that McClain would be a troublemaker. I don't think McClain set out to stir things up, but excitement sure has followed on his heels. If it turns out Lenny was killed because of that little bit of money from the auction, this could turn into a Vickers curse. Coming on top of that skull we found."

"What have you learned about that?" Sarah Elizabeth asked.

"Nothing so far. Hard to tell much from so little."

"I can't believe you didn't stick around!" Sarah Elizabeth protested. "What if they've got the whole skeleton there?

You'll miss the unveiling."

"Oh, I'll be back out there tomorrow," Delia promised her. "Besides, I doubt they'll find any more of him. Her. It. A few years ago a skull turned up not far from there when somebody was plowing his field. Just the skull, which probably got separated from the rest of its parts ages ago. You know, right here on the river, we're all walking over burial sites and garbage dumps left over from Paleo-Indian settlements."

Sarah Elizabeth frowned. "Am I supposed to know about that, too?" A relative newcomer to town, Sarah Elizabeth had been struggling to appreciate her own ancestral history, but enough was enough. "Paleo-whatchits can't possibly have pedigree charts. At least, I hope not. I mean, what's the point of knowing who your 25th great-grandmother was, anyway?"

"Eleanor of Aquitaine," Delia replied. "My 25th great-grandmother. And the point of knowing it is that I can impress people who don't do family research and don't know that Eleanor was the ancestor of just about everybody in the western hemisphere."

"In that case," Sarah Elizabeth said, greatly cheered, "I'll say she's mine, too. Who'll know the difference?"

"Frankie Mae would know, so don't try it on her." Delia edged closer to the glassed-in room which held the records she needed. "But right now I want to know about the Vickers family. McClain is seriously interested in the history of his house, and I'm hoping for an impressive bit of information that will guarantee he keeps the old place instead of tearing it down."

"Oh, but he was making definite plans to restore it," Sarah Elizabeth reminded her. "I don't think there's anything to worry about."

"Not right now," Delia agreed. "But wait until he finds out how much trouble it is to bring that dump up to code. Not to mention how much it'll cost him. Or maybe he'll be the one to decide there's a curse on the place and get out to avoid it. With luck, I'll find evidence that Queen Victoria slept there."

"You think?" Sarah Elizabeth asked.

Delia shook her head. Sarah Elizabeth had made great

strides, but she still had a long journey ahead of her.

Letting herself out of the office, Delia moved eagerly on to the genealogy section. She looked first at the census records for 1880, the first census taken after Jeremiah Vickers came to Jesus Creek. It was possible that he'd run screaming back to Boston within weeks, so before she wasted effort on him, she wanted to be sure he'd stayed around long enough to get noticed.

She'd copied the original census records herself, arranging them alphabetically—no small task—and thank goodness for that! In no time at all, Delia established that Jeremiah Vickers had, indeed, been living in Jesus Creek during the 1880 census. What's more, he'd been head of a household and married, to boot.

No doubt the wedding had taken place in Jesus Creek, so there were marriage indexes and possibly birth records to help. Newspapers and cemetery records were at hand, too. Delia dove headfirst into the nineteenth century and didn't come up for air until Sarah Elizabeth tapped on the door and announced closing time.

"You won't believe it!" Delia said breathlessly, clutching at scribbled notes as she waited for Sarah Elizabeth to lock up.

"Try me," the librarian challenged. "People come out of that genealogy room with all kinds of wild tales."

"Jeremiah Vickers didn't build the Vickers house!" Delia was ecstatic. "He bought it! And the previous owner was the widow Turner, his landlady."

Sarah Elizabeth pocketed the key and headed for her car. "I'll give you a ride," she offered. "So he rented before he bought? Is that important?"

"He didn't rent; he boarded. Now Jeremiah was married less than two years after he arrived in Jesus Creek, and he bought the Turner home. From his memoirs, I gather he wasn't much of a ladies' man, and Mrs. Turner appeared desperate to nab herself a son-in-law. Aha."

"Aha," Sarah Elizabeth agreed. "How does this help?"

Delia had forgotten she was talking to a new and reluctant

family researcher. She'd have to explain, step by step, the reason for her excitement. "I haven't found a marriage record yet, but I'll bet good money that Jeremiah Vickers married Mary Turner."

"Well," Sarah Elizabeth said cheerfully as she pulled the car into Delia's driveway, "now you're cookin'."

"Sarcasm isn't becoming," Delia reminded her. "Now I can follow Jeremiah back through Boston, if that seems interesting enough. More importantly, I know he's connected to the Turners. And I have, in his own words, a contemporary account of the Vickers place. I guarantee I'll find something in his memoirs to impress Dan McClain."

Delia accepted Sarah Elizabeth's weak smile for what it was—sincere congratulations from a young woman who hadn't a clue what the achievement meant.

Memoirs of Jeremiah Vickers, chapter 9, page 212

Mr. Howard and I retired to the back porch, where a gentle breeze did what it could to cleanse away the heat of the day. Dusk was still sometime distant, but in the valley where we resided, the evening often cooled to provide welcome relief from the endless daytime hours.

We gentlemen, however, were not outdoors to enjoy a leisurely respite. We had taken refuge there and cowered like frightened puppies. For the second time in a week, Miss Turner had dropped of a dead faint. Her mother and sister set briskly about restoring the stricken woman, employing smelling salts and a cool compress.

"Why do you suppose," Mr. Howard asked me, "we fear such a little thing? Why do we prefer this exile when those two ladies merely perform the necessary tasks?"

I had no answer, but attempted to analyze the circumstances. "There is a mystery to women," I said. "My own mother is beset by these spells upon occasion, and I have never fully grown accustomed to it. The weakness of women is nothing to fear; why, then, do we run from its symptoms?"

Howard gazed off into the distance, contemplating the question. When at last he spoke, his voice was soft, almost mournful. "I know little of weak women. I have had the good fortune to have been raised by a woman whose strength is unmatched by any man. My wife is very nearly her equal."

This confession stunned me, for I could not imagine the confident Mr. Howard playing henpecked husband. "Does it not . . . concern you?" I asked. "To spend your life with a woman who doesn't depend upon you? A woman who might do anything of her own accord and for her own reasons?"

Mr. Howard turned to me, a broad grin on his face. "It's fearfully frightening!" he admitted. "All the same, I find it a convenient circumstance. Business often calls me away, yet I never worry, for Mrs. Howard is capable of running our home and tending to matters of business that might arise in my absence."

"Naturally, Mrs. Howard, being indebted to you through marriage, is compelled to do what she can. But surely she'd rather you remain at home to carry the burden." I suspected, but did not say aloud, that his wife must grow weary of filling an unnatural role. Such mental exhaustion is known to produce in women—including my widowed mother—an uncertain temper, and forces them to make unreasonable demands upon their loved ones.

"Ours was a lengthy courtship," Mr. Howard explained. "She came to know me well, and yet was brave enough to accept me as a husband. I like to believe that her affection for me is as great as mine for her, and therefore a fair trade for the sacrifice. My advice is this, Mr. Vickers: find yourself a strong-willed woman. At best, she'll shoulder part of your burden, thus easing the journey of this life. At worst, she'll speak her mind and you'll waste no time wondering where you stand."

CHAPTER SEVEN

DELIA HAD PLANNED TO SPEND an hour or two at home, sorting through her notes and Jeremiah's memoirs before paying her respects to Lodina. Instead she'd caught herself pacing back and forth in the living room.

Her mind jumped from the mystery of Jeremiah to the mystery of Lenny's murder. Before she could pin down a full thought on either of those subjects, the skull found at the Vickers place would beckon.

Her living room was small; she couldn't pace more than four or five steps before turning. Pretty soon she was dizzy as well as frustrated. The obvious solution, Delia concluded, was to find more space to pace. She set out for a stroll, with no particular destination planned, and shortly thereafter found herself at the diner.

Eloise's Diner was nearly empty of customers when Delia arrived. Only Frank Pate, owner of Pate's Hardware Store, sat at his usual table next to the cash register. Like a warm country kitchen, Eloise's drew people to it; and in return, the diner provided customers a full stomach, good company, and a sense of belonging. It was, more than anyplace else, the heart of Jesus Creek.

"I can't get over it," Eloise said as soon as Delia sat down. "Good old Lenny Hemby. Remember when we had that big rain one summer a while back? Lenny was out in his little flat-bottom boat all day, rescuing folks in the flood zone. It's always a shame to lose somebody, but especially the good ones."

By this time the news of Lenny's death had spread throughout the town and across the county. Delia had expected that it would. That topic was, quite naturally, the first one Eloise wanted to discuss.

"I know," Delia agreed. "A few years ago when Roger and I made a trip to the Smokies, Lenny just took it on himself to mow my yard. He even trimmed around the edges of the house and deadheaded the petunias. Best my yard's ever looked."

"That was Lenny," Eloise sighed. "The Good Do-Bee of Jesus Creek."

"Have you heard any more about what happened?" Delia asked.

Eloise shook her big blonde hair; not a single strand moved. "Reb got a hamburger and fries to go, and lit out. I called Kay at home, but she's got her answering machine on, so either she's not there or she doesn't want to talk to me."

"Reb may have her working," Delia suggested. "He's had a busy day and Kay is the best help he's got."

"He'll run her to death!" Eloise protested. "Never gives her any time to spend with Wayne. How come Reb can't call German or Bernie to work overtime?"

"Do I have to explain it to you?" Delia asked. It was a rhetorical question, of course. The other police officers in Jesus Creek, German and Bernie, were both bigger and stronger than Kay; German was the more experienced officer, and Bernie, full of enthusiasm if not smarts, was better at following orders. But when a case required attention to detail and clear thought processes, Reb's only option was Kay Martin.

True, Kay could go off on a tangent, and goodness knows the girl has a mouth on her. All the same, she had found a balance between intuition and logic that served her—and the police department—quite well.

"Besides," Delia recounted, "Kay was first on the scene. She got the call because Reb was out at the Vickers place and his beeper wasn't on."

Eloise propped a hand on her womanly hip. "Delia Cannon, you're gettin' to be almost as good as me. How'd you come to know all that?"

"I was riding back with Reb from the Vickers place when—"

"I knew you'd be in on it," Eloise said with satisfaction. She delivered a glass of iced tea to Delia's table, then plunked down in the empty chair. "You've got a knack."

"For finding bodies?" Delia asked. "Don't be silly. It's only happened once before—"

"I meant for being where the excitement is. But you oughta be more careful who you hang around with. For all you know, this McClain person is a serial killer. Could've been burying his victims out there for years."

"Surely he'd have waited until after he bought the property to start hiding evidence," Delia reasoned. "The thing's been there quite a while, and it may have washed up during a flood in the last century."

"You sure this McClain's not a danger? Good. Then tell me more about him." Eloise leaned back, prepared to listen for as long as it took. "We're remarkably shy of eligible bachelors around here."

Delia was only surprised that Eloise had to ask for details. The old joke had been modified locally: There are three ways to spread the news—telephone, television, and t'Eloise. The grande dame of Jesus Creek, Eloise spent ten or twelve hours a day behind the counter at her diner, listening to customers and offering them advice and insight. Naturally she knew everything that went on in the town, and fortunately for gossip addicts like Delia, Eloise saw no reason to keep it to herself.

"He's been in here," Delia recapped. "You've met him, right?"

"Seen him," Eloise confirmed. "Chatted. Didn't learn a goldurned thing about him, though, besides the fact that he's a big sexy hunk and a mighty good tipper. What is he? CIA?"

Delia's mouth dropped open. "By george," she said, "Eloise, I think you've got it. That would explain why he's so closemouthed about his past, wouldn't it?"

"Could be in the witness protection program," offered Frank Pate, from across the room.

Delia nodded. "Could be. This will thrill Roger no end. I wonder what devious pranks he'll come up with to torment Mr. McClain."

On cue, Roger Shelton burst through the door, hauling a cardboard box in his arms. "Extra income for you, Eloise," he said and plunked the box on the counter beside the cash register.

"What on earth are you bringin' in here for me to have to throw out?" Eloise stood up and offered her chair to Roger, then stepped to the counter for a peek inside the box. "Rocks and twigs?"

Roger grinned with pride. "A rare and special gift, my dear. You can retire on the money you'll make from those items."

"Rocks and twigs," Eloise repeated. "What are you up to?"

"Ah, but not your average rocks and twigs," Roger assured her. "These all bear the unique signature of a neutrino-driven exhaust from one of the alien ships that landed in the woods near here."

Eloise reached inside the box and gingerly pulled out a medium-sized stone that appeared normal in every way. "I don't see—"

"Of course not. You don't have the trained eye." Roger helped himself to Delia's tea before explaining. "These were collected by the mayor's search team. Thoroughly checked out with a device that looks very like a metal detector, but modified—so I'm told—to pick up neutrino trails. Don't argue, Eloise. Just sell the darned things to tourists and give a percentage to the Extraterrestrial Observer Task Force."

Eloise shrugged and pulled a marking pen from her pocket. "A dollar each, you think?" she asked and proceeded to write that price on the side of the box. "Ten percent to the mayor and his vigilant boys."

"Betcha didn't know," said Frank Pate from the corner table, "that they got a new computer thingy down at the PD. It's hooked up to one of them gover'ment agencies that looks for alien signals."

"Know about it?" Roger asked. "Why, my friend, I suggested it!"

Delia didn't doubt for a moment that he spoke the truth. Early retirement had been a very bad idea in Roger's case. It left him with far too much leisure time for getting into trouble. Or stirring it up.

At least he'd had the good fortune to move to Jesus Creek shortly thereafter, though; egging on the other residents in whatever half-baked schemes they came up with kept Roger busy and off the streets. The amazing thing to her was that Roger had gotten into the Zen of Jesus Creek within moments of his arrival there, whereas she—a lifelong resident—still struggled to make sense of the goings-on in the town. "What sort of computer did you sell the PD?" she asked, only mildly alarmed.

"No, no," Roger said quickly. "It's the same old computer. We've just added software. Al downloaded it from the Internet, didn't cost a thing. It analyzes data that's been collected by the Arecibo radio telescope."

"Oh, and the government knows about this?" Now Delia was alarmed. "Don't you think they might object to having their data stolen by—"

"You wound me!" Roger slapped a hand to his chest, somewhere in the vicinity of his heart. "SETI—that's the Search for Extraterrestrial Intelligence to the uninitiated—has asked for volunteers to help them. I'm not making this up."

Delia was sure he was telling the truth, because Roger didn't lie. He sometimes omitted details and he frequently twisted words to make the truth sound like something else, but he didn't lie.

"Here, Delia." Eloise gave her a fresh glass of iced tea. "Maybe that's why the CIA man is here. Maybe he's keeping an eye on this computer, just in case the mayor and Al know more than's good for 'em."

"CIA?" Roger turned to Delia for clarification. "We've got CIA in town?"

Delia reached across the table, gently took Roger's hand in hers, and dug her fingernails into his palm. "No," she said.

"No CIA?" Roger pouted.

"I don't know whether he's CIA or not, but no, you are not

going to start up with that. Stick to aliens. They won't hurt you as badly."

"Could be," Frank Pate offered, "this McClain is an alien."

"I don't think the CIA employs aliens," Eloise mentioned.

"McClain is an alien?" Roger asked. He pulled his hand free and glared at Delia. "And you didn't report this right away? I'll have to put your name on my List of Suspicious Persons."

Delia closed her eyes and massaged her temples. "I am getting a terrible headache," she explained. "It happens every time I fall through the hole into this dimension. Please send me back to my own world, where conversations are linear and people are sane."

"I'll get you a salad," Eloise promised and disappeared into the kitchen. "You've probably just got a hunger headache."

"Why does Eloise think McClain is an alien?" Roger asked.

"Because she's been around you too much. May I please tell you what happened today? Without interruption?" Delia pleaded.

Roger sat back in his chair, folding his hands in his lap. "Yes, my love. Tell me about your day."

As succinctly as possible, Delia explained the Historical Society's visit to the Vickers house, McClain's apparent interest in preserving the property, and the unexpected discovery in the backyard. Roger listened intently, keeping quiet even when Delia paused to allow him a frivolous remark. "Reb and I were just coming back into town when Kay flagged us down. That's how I found out about Lenny."

It was Frank Pate who interrupted the narrative. "I wouldn't be surprised if it turns out that old man Vickers buried somebody in his yard," he offered.

"Why's that?" Delia asked. "Did he sell cemetery plots?"

"Naw. But he disappeared, you know. Just up and vanished. Left Dot and the kids to fend for themselves. Maybe he was running from the law."

Eloise returned then with Delia's salad and a plate of biscuits for Roger. "If Pete Vickers was gonna kill somebody, it would've been that wife of his," she said firmly.

"Mary Gale?" Frank asked. "Well, she did die awful young, didn't she?"

"Not her." Eloise shook her head. "That Dot Hemby he married after Mary Gale passed on."

"Hold the phone!" Roger rolled his eyes in frustration. "I'm new here. Somebody give me the tale in chronological order, please."

Eloise leaned against the counter and wiped her hands on her apron. "First Pete Vickers married Mary Gale . . . Something. I was just a baby when she died. I don't remember her maiden name. She wasn't from around here. Then Mary Gale died and Pete remarried to Dot Hemby—the one who just died a while back—who was a widow with two young kids. Then Pete up and disappeared, leaving Dot with that farm out there which promptly went to hell in a handbasket because she had no money and no help except for her kids, who were fairly young at the time and pretty much useless for helping around the farm. By the time they grew up, neither one of them wanted to keep a farm."

Roger took a moment to process the information, then nodded to signal he was ready for more. "So Pete Vickers is the bad guy, because he ran out on his wife."

"No, Pete's a victim of a foul-tempered woman is how I figure it," Eloise insisted.

"Unless he killed somebody and had to leave town," Frank added. "Or maybe he worked for the CIA, too, and he's gone undercover."

"Did Pete's father own the land before him?" Delia asked. She was determined to get some piece of worthwhile information from the conversation.

"Sure," Eloise said. "It's not like Pete could've afforded to buy all that. It's been Vickers land for as long as I can remember."

"Except when it became Hemby land after Dot died," Frank reminded her.

"Shoot, the Hemby kids owned it just long enough to sell it."

"Do either of you remember the name Jeremiah Vickers?"

Delia asked.

Frank and Eloise thought it over. "No," they finally agreed.

"There was Pete and, before that, his daddy," Eloise elaborated. "I don't remember his daddy's name, though. That was before I was born. Long before."

"I wonder," Delia said, "if Lodina would know anything. Maybe Pete Vickers would have mentioned his family, his ancestors—"

"Well, I can tell you right now, Lodina wouldn't have paid attention even if it'd been talked about. She was just a kid when Pete took off. Probably don't even remember him." Eloise was unaware that she'd thrown a bucket of ice water on Delia's hopes.

"I've never heard of any other Vickers family around here, have you?" Delia asked. "And I've got this manuscript written by a Jeremiah Vickers in the late 1800s. He moved here from up north, so it seems likely he started the Jesus Creek line, and it appears he was the first Vickers to live in that house, so he'd almost certainly be an ancestor to Pete Vickers."

"Okay, but that wouldn't make him kin to the Hemby kids," Eloise pointed out.

"No," Delia agreed, "but Dan McClain plans to restore the old house. You know I'm in favor of that. I'm trying to get some history on the place, just in case McClain's enthusiasm for the project wanes. Something that would make the place too interesting to tear down. Just anything I could pass on to McClain."

"Why don't you make something up?" Eloise suggested. "It's not like he'd know the difference."

"Ethics," Delia said sadly. "Unfortunately, I have ethics."

"You know who could tell you about Pete?" Frank said suddenly. "Miss Constance Winter. She'd remember him, for sure."

Delia's confidence was not so great as Frank's. "Miss Constance is crazy. She's been crazy since the day she was born. It's a tradition in the Winter family."

"Still and all, she'd know."

"I don't suppose it would hurt to ask her," Delia decided.

"Sure, sweetie," Roger agreed. "Maybe Miss Constance has a message for me, too. You know, she's in constant contact with Zetron, leader of the High Command from Plesauius, the third planet in the Alpha Centauri system. Ask her about her abduction. It's a very interesting twist on the usual taken-to-the-mothership story."

Delia wasn't the least bit surprised to hear this. "Tomorrow, though. We've got a more important event tonight."

Roger fairly beamed. "That's right! Your first computer lesson."

For once, Delia didn't have to make up an excuse. "Sorry, dear, but we'll have to put that off. Tonight we're going to Lodina's to pay our respects."

There was a moment of hesitation from Roger. Delia knew he'd prefer to avoid the unpleasant fact of Lenny's death and Lodina's mourning—for that matter, so would she—but he understood that certain customs had to be observed and he would not argue. "Yes, okay," he relented. "You'll expect me to wear a suit, but can I at least wear my Marvin the Martian tie?"

"Absolutely not!" Delia, Eloise, and Frank shouted it in unison.

"But Lenny liked Marvin," Roger insisted.

Putting her hands on her hips, Eloise explained in no uncertain terms, "It doesn't matter what Lenny liked. He's gone, and we'll all show our respect by dressing like decent folks."

"But—" Roger tried again.

"Give it up, Roger," Delia advised. "Rules are rules, even the unwritten ones."

Roger dropped Delia at home before driving to his apartment to shower and to change into the dark suit he kept on hand for weddings and funerals. "I'll be back in an hour," he told her. "Will you be ready?"

"Of course I will," she promised. "One hour." The minute she saw his car turn the corner, Delia grabbed the memoirs. Just a few pages, she told herself, while the bathtub is filling.

Jeremiah, squeezed between the Turner sisters, had prayed hard for his life all the way into town, as Clarissa held the reins. She drove the wagon with a great deal more confidence and enthusiasm than Jeremiah felt was due.

Mary Turner, long accustomed to her sister's driving, had had the foresight to cover her face with a sheer scarf to protect it from sun and swirling dust. In addition, she made use of an attractive yet functional parasol. (Clarissa, as usual, had ventured out with only a frill of a bonnet to shade her face.)

As soon as the wagon came to a halt, Clarissa hopped lightly to the ground. "I'm going directly to the General Store," she announced, "and I'll be there until I find a proper pair of church gloves."

She set off at a brisk pace, leaving Jeremiah to climb cautiously from the wagon and help Mary to the ground. Unlike the disturbingly energetic Clarissa, they both needed a minute to tuck and straighten and generally regain their equilibrium.

Accustomed to milder climes, Jeremiah was lightheaded from the combination of heat and speed, and now discretely used his handkerchief to mop grime and perspiration from his flushed face. He thoroughly regretted having agreed to Mrs. Turner's request that he accompany her daughters into town.

"I worry so," she'd said. "It will be a comfort to me to know that they have your protection." Jeremiah saw no way to turn away from such a heartfelt plea, even though he wondered what escort had been provided for the daughters in the many years before his presence.

"Not many about in town today," Mary commented idly.

Jeremiah surveyed the area. In the heart of Jesus Creek, a dozen and more horses were tied at posts but pedestrians were few. The same boy he'd met before squatted in the shade of the tavern's awning, holding Red Fox with one hand and practicing marbles with the other. *What sort of business required Mr. Howard's presence in the tavern?* Jeremiah wondered.

Aside from the boy, only two other souls were out in the day's heat—trail hands, by the look of them, engaged in conversation a few feet away. They glanced briefly in Jeremiah's direction, dismissed him, then turned away to continue their talk.

It was no great task to deduce that the bulk of citizens lounged inside Delia's Tavern. A buzz of voices, along with the *plink-plink* of a badly tuned piano, drifted through the open door of the saloon. An occasional hoot suggested that someone was winning at cards, yet another pastime which won no favor with Jeremiah.

"I'll be a moment in the bank, and then I'll collect supplies from Mr. Mooten, as I'm sure Clarissa won't have remembered that's our purpose here. She has no gift for the running of a household." Mary frowned, then glanced at Jeremiah as if hoping he would agree.

"I'll accompany you, then, if there's no objection," he offered. In truth he'd have preferred to avoid conversation with the banker, who chattered like a chipmunk when there was business to be done. On the other hand, the bank's interior was likely to be somewhat cooler than the sidewalk, and there was no way of knowing who might stumble out of the tavern across the road. It wasn't a difficult choice.

Jeremiah pushed open the door, then stepped back to allow Mary to precede him into the bank. As soon as he'd cleared the threshold and before his sunstruck eyes grew accustomed to the dark interior, the door was rudely slammed behind him.

"Stand where you are!" The command was shouted into Jeremiah's ear. It was a pointless order. The gun pressed against his cheek kept the schoolmaster glued to the spot on which he stood. He could not have moved, in any case, because his nerves had deserted his body. Jeremiah wasn't even certain that he breathed. Ahead of him, Mary Turner stood equally paralyzed, although her face expressed more annoyance and disapproval than fear.

"Hurry it up!" The gunman at the door called to his

partner.

Behind the desk, Mr. Thurston Byrd, head clerk of the Jesus Creek Bank, stood by helplessly as the second robber shoved cash into a grain sack. Byrd's small eyes darted from the outlaw nearest him to Mary and Jeremiah. Perhaps he would have put up some resistance, but certainly not now, not while the ruffian pointed a revolver at the innocent young woman.

The robber at the cash drawer swept the last of the coins into his sack. A kerchief covered the lower half of his face, but above that his eyes crinkled with laughter as he turned to his partner. "A good haul," he said. Then, with extraordinary calm and with barely a glance at the clerk, he put his revolver to Thurston Byrd's head and pulled the trigger.

The banker's corpse fell unceremoniously across the desk; at the same time, Mary Turner slumped to the floor with a solid thud. For a moment Jeremiah feared the bullet had somehow exited through Byrd and murdered the young woman, but a slight wheeze and whistle from her assured him that the lady had only fainted.

Jeremiah wished for the same oblivion! Instead he stood alone, forced to watch as the cold-hearted killers of the poor banker made away with their loot.

The gunman nearest the door pressed his revolver harder against Jeremiah's cheek and chuckled.

"Leave 'im!" ordered the other, the one who had shot Byrd. "He's nothing of a threat, no more than the woman." To Jeremiah he said, "Your luck is high today. You ain't dead, and you can brag that it was Jesse James himself who let you live."

CHAPTER EIGHT

LODINA HEMBY LANE would have a hissy fit once daylight broke and she was able to see the damage done to her yard. Dozens of cars were parked on the lawn; some of them trampled Lodina's randomly placed flower beds, and all would surely leave ruts in the soft ground.

Lenny had been a friend to everyone in Jesus Creek, and it seemed they were all paying their respects at the same time. In addition to cars squeezed into the yard door handle to door handle, other vehicles lined both sides of the street for as far as Delia could see. Several of them had parked in Delia's yard, too.

"You'd think it was a party!" Roger grumbled.

Delia, decked out in a respectable gray suit and heels that were not made for walking, had to agree. "I didn't expect a full turnout tonight," she admitted. "Isn't anybody waiting for the official viewing?"

The funeral home wouldn't have Lenny's body prepared until late the next day. In the meantime, friends and neighbors gathered at Lodina's house to offer support and provide solace in the form of comfort food. Whether the grieving sister felt up to entertaining—well, that mattered not a whit. Ritual takes precedence over mere human preference.

"Remind me to clean house before you die," Delia said as she and Roger stepped out the door.

A biting wind cut through her dress coat as they hurried across the yard toward Lodina's house. Roger carried his famous green bean casserole, while Delia coddled a double-chocolate fudge cake she'd purchased from Eloise. "I don't cook for the living," she'd said often, "why should I cook for the dead?"

They reached Lodina's front porch at the same time as three other people (ham sandwiches, red velvet cake, and macaroni-cheese casserole), and the five of them pushed through the door without knocking.

Lodina's small foyer led to the dining room on the right, where two dozen mourners circled the loaded table. The crowd moved slowly, each one contentedly filling a plate from the enormous potluck offering.

The house, though no larger than Delia's, was considerably more decorated. Lodina's taste in furnishing ran to dark reproductions of the Victorian style. Stark white walls made the heavy, ornate furniture stand out like neon glow tubes, though, Delia reflected.

To the left of the foyer was an equally crowded living room. Over-perfumed matrons, stuffed into wool suits, were crammed three to the sofa and two to each chair. Several were forced to stand in corners, each awaiting her turn to be useful. Lodina huddled in a velvet wing chair, oblivious to the stout woman who rubbed Lodina's arms with more enthusiasm than purpose.

"She'll peel the skin off that poor woman," Roger said, taking the cake from Delia.

He ran interference and cleared a path to the dining room, where Patricia Patrick, self-appointed hostess, greeted them with hearty hugs, careful not to upset the food he carried.

"Here," she said. "Let me put that cake on the kitchen counter, Roger, and just set your casserole on the table, anywhere you can find a spot."

"How's Lodina?" Delia asked, as Roger relinquished the chocolate cake. She followed Patricia into the next room, but there was no relief from the mourners there. Every inch of floor was taken up by people who'd already filled their plates and now struggled to eat while being jostled by newcomers.

Patricia grabbed a knife and sliced the cake into generous portions. "Doing as well as can be expected," she said with a heavy sigh. "The poor old thing has to bear so much."

Given that Lodina and Patricia were of a similar age, Delia

assumed that "old thing" was a term of affection. "I gather Reb hasn't made any progress."

Patricia shook her head. "Not so far as I know." She dropped her voice a notch before adding, "I can't imagine it! What sort of person just breaks into a man's house and shoots him in cold blood?"

Delia could imagine it, unfortunately. But then, she was far more cynical about the nature of humanity than was sweet and perky Patricia. Instead of explaining, she turned to check on Roger and found him stalled in the dining room, engaged in intense conversation with Henry Mooten.

Despite his natural irreverence, Roger could usually be counted on to behave respectably at such times. Usually. Delia decided it was safe to leave him in the care of Henry for a few minutes more while she fulfilled her duties to the next of kin. "I'd better say hello to Lodina," she told Patricia.

Patricia licked a blob of fudge frosting from her finger. "Do that, hon. Then come back and get a bite to eat. She'll be so glad to see you."

Delia doubted that Lodina would have any feeling at all about her presence, but propriety demanded certain actions and responses. Delia understood the rules of grief etiquette, but unlike Patricia, she'd never taken them to heart.

Delia made her way to the living room, greeted folks in passing, and wished she'd sent a nice bouquet instead of showing up in person. She found Lodina in the same spot as before, still surrounded by hovering concern and looking no more comforted than she had earlier. "Lodina, hon," Delia said and leaned forward to hug the shriveled and grief-stricken woman.

Lodina tried to rise from her chair, but one of the protectors pushed her firmly back into it. "Oh, Delia!" Lodina's voice was nearly a whimper. "It's so awful! I pray you never have to go through this."

Delia hoped her friend's prayers carried some weight. "You know Roger and I are here if you need us," she said sincerely. Although she'd never once been called upon to perform any significant task for the bereaved, Delia always made the polite offer.

"Would you just walk around with me a bit?" Lodina asked. This time she got to her feet and forced her way past the friends who would have coddled her endlessly. "My butt's numb from sitting, and I feel like I ought to be doing something."

Delia took Lodina's arm and together they pushed through the room. As the two women moved into the foyer, the front door opened to admit a blast of chilly air along with Dan McClain.

For one frozen second, Dan appeared stunned, as if he hadn't expected to find anyone home. Then he closed the door firmly behind him and looked directly into Lodina's strained face. "Mrs. Lane," he said. "You may not remember me. Dan McClain."

"Well, how nice of you." Lodina wrapped stiff arms around him to simulate a hug.

Delia thought McClain flinched, but she suspected that was a reaction to Lodina's too-sweet perfume. Possibly he just didn't take to being embraced by strangers. Delia, not a huggy person herself, could understand that.

"It's kind of you to be here," Delia said, and she meant it. She made no effort to touch McClain, not even to shake hands.

"Please help yourself to the food," Lodina urged. "There's more than an army could eat."

McClain nodded and hurried into the dining room, as if he'd suddenly decided he wanted nothing to do with Lodina. He made no eye contact along the way, and no one spoke to him, although the conversational hum quickly turned to a buzz.

"I don't know what it is about that man," Lodina said quietly, once McClain was out of the foyer, "but he gives me the willies."

Delia caught herself rubbing Lodina's arm and quickly pulled her hand away, hoping Roger hadn't seen. "Maybe it's because he bought your homeplace," she suggested. "Like a psychological invasion."

Lodina waved that away. "I never had any love for that old shack. I hated it from the minute we first moved there, and all I ever thought about was getting away. Of all the men on earth, my mama had to pick a farmer." Lodina sighed. "Of course, Mama was out of the same cloth."

"Oh, Pete Vickers was really a farmer?" Delia asked. "I thought he might have had some other job and just held on to the land."

Lodina rolled her eyes. "All that man knew was how to dig in the dirt. That was all he did, all he talked about, and all he cared about."

"It must have put a burden on your mother when she was left to run the place by herself," Delia said. "Why didn't y'all ever sell it and move back to town?"

Lodina shrugged and started moving through the house again. "Just one of those things," she said vaguely.

"Well, if it makes you feel any better," Delia added, "Mr. McClain has a real mess on his hands now. I don't know if you've heard—the landscapers turned up a partial burial while they were digging a pond."

Confusion replaced the strain on Lodina's face. "What pond?"

Delia quickly outlined the morning's events for Lodina. "I'm afraid they may have run across some family grave sites."

"Not *my* family," Lodina assured her. "There's no telling what those Vickers people might've done with their dead."

The genealogist in Delia jumped forward. "Was it a big family? How many Vickerses did you know?"

As much as Delia's interest had peaked, Lodina's ebbed. "Just my stepfather," she said without enthusiasm. "I don't recall meeting a one of 'em. Mama never had anything to do with his kin when he was around, and certainly not after he ran off and left us."

"Pete Vickers just disappeared, right?" Delia shook her head. "That's odd behavior for a responsible, dedicated farmer."

Lodina shrugged. "He headed out to California for whatever reason. To get rich, I guess. Who knows what goes on in a man's mind?"

Delia wasn't surprised that Lodina had such a low opinion of men, not after the way her husband had treated her. Before that, Lodina's male role models had included a father who'd died while she was an infant, and a stepfather who'd deserted his family in order to chase after fool's gold.

The crowd at the food bank had changed components, but the size remained the same. "Let me fix you a plate," Delia suggested, suddenly desperate to comfort Lodina in any way she could.

"Oh, no." Lodina pressed a wadded handkerchief to her mouth. "I don't want food. I just want this all to be over with."

Delia put an arm around Lodina's shoulders and steered her down the hallway. "Go into the bathroom for a minute," she instructed. "Lock the door, keep the lights off, and ignore all this out here. Patricia knows how to run the show, and you deserve a break."

Lodina obeyed without a word of protest. "I'm so tired of carrying on," she whispered.

As soon as the door closed behind her, Lodina began to sob. Delia's heart ached, but she knew it was best to leave Lodina alone. Let her get a little of it out of her system, Delia thought.

She found Patricia still choreographing traffic, slicing desserts, and tidying up used plates and glassware. "Lodina's on her last nerve," Delia said.

"Don't I know?" For a minute, Patricia stopped fiddling about and looked directly at Delia. "I've never seen a brother and sister as close as those two were," she said. "Honestly, I don't know what Lodina will do now. They've leaned on each other ever since they were kids."

"But they both married," Delia reminded her. "They weren't together so much then."

"As good as," Patricia said. "I remember Caroline was jealous of Lodina. She implied some terrible things, you know. Couldn't understand that Lenny just genuinely loved his sister."

"Do you think that contributed to the divorce?" Delia asked.

"To Lenny's, maybe." Patricia snatched up a dirty plate which had been deposited by a guest. "The only thing that contributed to Lodina's divorce was that tramp Jim took up with."

This was a road Delia didn't want to travel at that moment, so she quickly changed the subject. "It's a shame Lodina never was close to her stepfather's people," she said. "She might've had some of them to help her through this."

Patricia nodded in agreement. "I can't imagine what that man must've been thinking. If he knew he was going to run off and leave his family, why did he marry Dot in the first place?"

"Maybe we can find out what became of Pete Vickers," Delia said. The thought had just occurred to her, and she was barely aware that she spoke aloud.

"You think he became a millionaire? If so, Lodina sure ought to sue him for some of his money." Patricia turned to search for more dishes to clean. "Lodina!" she cried, looking past Delia toward the hallway.

Delia spun around, expecting the worst. Instead she saw Lodina standing in the doorway and clutching at the frame for support. Her swollen eyes stared straight ahead as if she were in a trance.

Patricia and Delia rushed to her side, reenacting their earlier rescue. Step by step, they guided Lodina back down the hallway and deposited her on a bed covered in pillows and pink ruffles. Delia picked up a matching pink mohair afghan and spread it over Lodina after Patricia had removed her shoes.

"You stay right here," Patricia said. "I'm going to fix up a plate of food and feed it to you myself, if that's what it takes. You haven't eaten a bite since this morning. It's no wonder you look so peaked."

Leading Delia from the room, Patricia shut the door gently behind her. "You see what I'm talking about?" she whispered.

"I'm afraid to leave her alone. There's no telling what might happen."

"Delia, the mayor has an explanation." Roger grabbed her as she returned to the dining room and pulled her into a cluster that included Henry Mooten, Reb Gassler, and Dan McClain.

"An explanation for what?" Delia asked fearfully.

Henry was clearly revved up about something, Reb was in a state of amused detachment, and Dan McClain appeared to be part of the group by accident and· paid more attention to the new vinyl flooring than to the conversation.

"That skull," Henry said. "Did you notice anything funny about it?"

"I'm not an expert on these things," Delia said, hoping Henry wouldn't pursue the questioning.

"Like it being sort of pointed at the top?" Henry pushed his glasses farther up his nose. "Because I wouldn't be surprised to learn it's an alien that crashed out there. Maybe around the same time as the Roswell crash."

"Now that's Henry's theory," Roger explained. "Personally, I think it's human. Most likely the tragic result of alien experimentation."

While she recognized and appreciated that his alien fixation kept Roger off the street and out of bars, Delia knew that encouraging tales of terror in Jesus Creek was a bad thing. "It's an alien skull, Roger," she said firmly. "I saw it with my own eyes. No way it could be human."

Clearly disappointed, Roger pulled out his wallet and handed five dollars to Henry. "You win," he said. "May as well leave now, Delia. We'll talk about your traitorous behavior later."

"Hey," she said, "I call 'em like I see 'em."

By the time Delia retrieved her coat, both Roger and McClain had joined her in the foyer. No one noticed their departure, engrossed as they were in food and conversation. Not that Lodina would care, Delia thought, but it was a successful wake.

Outside, the temperature had dropped again and Roger swore he felt ice in the air. "February should be abolished," he insisted, shoving his hands into his pockets. "It serves no useful purpose, and it drags out the misery of winter."

"Valentine's Day," Delia reminded him. "Chocolate. A perfectly valid excuse for the rest of the month."

McClain hung like a shadow behind them, contributing nothing to the banter. If the cold night air bit at his face and ears, he gave no sign of it.

"I can't imagine what it must be doing to Lodina," Delia said as she stepped off the porch. "Lenny was probably the kindest, most gentle person this town has ever seen. Why would anyone want to hurt him?"

"Maybe he wasn't." It was the first time McClain had spoken since he'd greeted Lodina.

Roger and Delia turned to stare, waiting for Dan McClain to explain his cynical comment.

"Did you know Lenny?" Roger asked sharply.

"I talked with him briefly at the auction," McClain admitted.

"Then what is it that makes you think he deserved to die?" It was unlike Roger to get testy, especially with a near stranger. Another time, Delia would have chided him for his tone, if not his words. In this case, she decided Roger's snappish attitude was justified.

"Everyone has a dark side." McClain wasn't defensive; he merely explained his remark. "Everybody has a secret that not even his closest friends know about."

"So your idea about Lenny's hidden self is just a guess?" Roger pressed. "Or did it come up during your two-minute therapy session at the auction?"

"I only meant," McClain replied coolly, "that we never really know anyone."

Even though she also was angered by the outrageous suggestion, Delia wanted to defuse the tension that hung as thick as their breaths in the air. Lodina's front yard was no fit place for an argument, nor for a philosophical debate about the basic nature of mankind. "We should all get home," she said firmly. "Mr. McClain, I'll see you bright and early tomorrow morning." She didn't wait for—or expect—the boys to shake hands and make nice. Grabbing Roger's arm, Delia stalked across the yard toward her own house, dragging her beloved with her.

Roger didn't wait until they were inside to express his opinion. "Your new friend has a big mouth." He pushed open the front door and allowed Delia to pass in front of him. "And he's got more nerve than common sense."

"I'm not disagreeing with you, Roger." Delia kicked off her shoes. "He was out of line. Maybe that's considered appropriate funeral commentary where he comes from."

"And just where does he come from that he's never heard the old saying 'Don't speak ill of the dead'?" Roger ripped off his tie and tossed it on the floor beside Delia's high heels.

"Good question," she admitted. "Reb and I asked him outright, and he avoided the question."

Roger stopped loosening his clothes and gave her a steely look. "I don't like him," he said plainly. "And I don't trust him. I hope you've got your eyes open on this one."

Delia moved in closer, wrapping her arms around Roger and looking up into his face. "I don't think I trust him, either. But I won't let a little thing like that keep me out of my front-row seat at the excavation."

As soon as the robbers exited the bank, Jeremiah's knees gave way. Gasping for air, he crawled on all fours and leaned his ear to Mary's face. She was, indeed, breathing and would come round of her own accord in time. Sadly, there was nothing to be done for Thurston Byrd.

Pushing to his feet, Jeremiah staggered to the door, which he opened a mere crack. He peered outside and saw the robbers, already mounted, joined by the two trail hands he'd noticed earlier. Obviously those were the lookouts. The four members of the gang rode away at top speed as Jeremiah mentally thrashed himself for not having formed a suspicion earlier. If only he'd paid attention to the trail hands who stood there in the street, for no discernible purpose. If only he'd reported them to the sheriff. "If only," he said aloud, "if only."

The outlaws broke into groups, two riding off toward the west, the other two in the opposite direction. Jeremiah couldn't make out the killer—they all wore similar dusters—and in any case, they were near out of sight by the time it occurred to him that his identification might be useful when they were caught.

Jeremiah bolted from the bank and ran as fast as his wobbly legs would allow, straight to the most likely source of help. His chest felt as if it would explode, for there had been not a moment for drawing a full breath since he'd entered the bank.

After what seemed to him an eternity, he burst through the open door of Delia's Tavern. Words tumbled out of his mouth, high-pitched like a schoolgirl's, but loud enough to be heard above the rowdy din. "Robbed! The bank! Byrd dead! Help!"

The room fell silent; even the piano player stopped his abuse of the instrument. Every man in the place saw the wild-eyed terror on Jeremiah's face, but his words needed a few seconds to sink into their whiskey-fogged brains.

Sheriff Leach, who had been reclined against the bar, strode across the room and pushed through the crowd which surrounded Jeremiah. Putting first things first, he took Jeremiah's arm and led him to the nearest chair. "Sit here," the sheriff instructed. "Take your breath."

Inhalation wouldn't help, Jeremiah knew, but he did as told. "Mr. Byrd has been murdered, and Miss Turner is in a dead faint."

At these words, Dr. Savage bolted out of the saloon to provide assistance to the distressed lady. The others remained behind, eager for details of the crime.

"How many were there?" the sheriff asked.

Jeremiah held up four fingers. "Two inside and two keeping watch outside. I saw them when we arrived—the two on the street, that is—but paid no heed. They looked ordinary."

"What about the others?" the sheriff pressed. "Can you

give a fair description?"

Jeremiah shook his head. "The one was quite tall; the other, the killer, was my height. Both wore trail coats and covered their faces with kerchiefs. I confess that in my shock, I failed to notice details."

"Which way did they head out?" the sheriff asked. "Did you see anything?"

Thankful that he could finally provide much-needed information, Jeremiah described how the gang had split up and ridden away in opposite directions.

As soon as this was said, the sheriff raised a hand and waved toward the door. "Gather your arms and supplies! We'll ride in two groups. Stinger," he said, turning to a grizzled veteran, "you lead to the east. I'll take my men to the river."

There was sudden chaos as nearly every man in the place dashed away to form the posse. Delia Cannon's herd of strapping sons led the stampede, pushing aside smaller men in their eagerness for action. When the chaos died down, and Jeremiah at last had a moment to survey his surroundings, he found himself alone with the tavern owner and the four men who remained behind.

The piano player, Delia, and the barkeep all gazed as if he were a curious specimen in a traveling show; J. D. Howard's face showed him to be inexplicably amused; and from the darkest corner of the room, Elmer Winter glared at the schoolmaster as if he were a bug.

"Miss Delia." Howard rose from his seat—for he and the mad drunkard Winter had been the only customers who had not rushed to hear the tale—and made himself comfortable at Jeremiah's table. "A hearty drink for Mr. Vickers, if you will."

The barkeep had anticipated the request, and the order was filled almost immediately. "This will help," Delia said and put a full glass down in front of Jeremiah.

It was then that Clarissa crashed into the saloon, too alarmed to be ashamed at her presence in such a place. "Mr. Vickers! Oh, goodness. Are you injured?" she cried breathlessly.

Both Jeremiah and J. D. Howard rose, the former startled to his feet by the sudden appearance of a lady in the tavern.

"Sit here," Howard said to Clarissa, offering his chair. "Your sister is well, according to Mr. Vickers, and the doctor is with her."

Clarissa collapsed into the seat and studied Jeremiah's face. "I've already seen to Mary," she said. "The doctor says it's just another of her spells. Happens quite often, and the doctor already has her on her feet. She's in a temper, I can tell. It's a lucky thing for those bandits she isn't riding after them!"

Jeremiah was greatly relieved to learn that the young lady had suffered no lasting effects. He took up the beverage before him and gulped half the liquid before spewing it out again. "Agh! That isn't water!"

Putting a hand to her mouth, Delia feigned a cough to cover her laughter. Clarissa and Howard were not so gracious.

"The schoolmaster isn't prone to drink," Howard explained. "Mr. Vickers, sip a bit at first. The Lord will certainly forgive you for it. If ever you ought to abandon temperance, now is the time."

"That's the truth," Clarissa agreed. "And I won't say a word to Mother. In fact—" She grabbed up the glass and took a dainty swallow. "A little something for my nerves."

It was all too much for Jeremiah! Ruffians, robbery, murder, and now young ladies partaking of spirits inside the saloon. If his mother heard how life was lived on the frontier—well, it was best not to contemplate her reaction.

Suddenly Jeremiah chuckled. "To think I'm worried about the evils of drink after staring down the barrel of Jesse James's gun!"

"What's that you say about Jesse James?" Howard demanded.

"I've just told you how he robbed the bank." Jeremiah took a little of the whiskey and decided that it was, indeed, having a soothing effect.

"You never said it was the James boys," Howard replied, in

a calmer tone. "What gave you the idea just now?"

"Why, Jesse James himself!" Jeremiah declared in his own defense. "He introduced himself, just after his heinous crime."

"That puts a new spot on the leopard," Howard said, more to himself than to Jeremiah. Then, as if he'd debated for hours and finally reached a conclusion, J. D. Howard nodded firmly. "I believe I'll ride along with the posse, after all."

CHAPTER NINE

THE MORNING WAS CHILLY, but the weatherman promised "spring-like conditions" later in the day. Delia had little faith in meteorologists' predictions, however, and so she'd dressed in layers and tucked gloves and a pair of thick wool socks in her purse.

She stepped out the front door at the indecent hour of 7:00 A.M., willing to sacrifice her sleep in exchange for the excitement of skeletal excavation. Delia also hoped that she could cope with Miss Constance better if she weren't quite awake.

The sun was just topping the trees, and a pale haze hung in the air. Delia inhaled the heavy scent of hickory smoke in the morning air; one of her neighbors had just stoked a woodstove. The peaceful scene was made complete by the *clop-clop* of horse hooves on pavement.

Delia turned toward the sound and waved at Kay Martin as she approached on her official police department steed. Delia knew nothing about horses, but Kay insisted that Sundance was just a big old friendly palomino puppy. All the same, Delia waited beside her open car door, the better to make a quick getaway in case the animal went berserk.

"Have you called 911?" Kay asked as she and Sundance halted in Delia's yard. "I know there's a crisis, because you're out and about before noon."

"I'm an eccentric older woman," Delia said. "This is a ploy to confuse you all."

"It works." Kay dismounted and fed Sundance an apple slice, telling him he was a "Good boy. *Good* boy." Turning again to Delia, she asked, "Seriously. What's up?"

"I'm off to the excavation at the Vickers place," Delia said gleefully. "But first I have to pay a visit to Miss Constance."

Kay grimaced. "Don't mention my name. I owe her ten dollars from a poker game last month. I swear she cheats; I just haven't figured out how she does it."

"The aliens probably tell her what you're holding." Delia watched as Sundance deposited fertilizer on her lawn. "We went over to Lodina's last night," she went on. "She's not taking Lenny's death in stride."

"Reb told me," Kay said. "He's fairly torn up about it, too. Reb and Lenny were fishing buddies, you know. The TBI is doing all the usual poking round, and of course they want us to stay out of their way."

Delia grinned, imagining what Reb must think of that arrangement. "I suppose the TBI can't have it their way every time."

"I thought so, too," Kay said, "but Reb won't touch this one. He answers direct questions and he gave the TBI full access to everything they want, of course. But he flat refuses to investigate this one."

This news disturbed Delia. She'd known Reb Gassler all her life, and he was the closest a mortal came to being a Defender of Truth and Justice. Was he burned out? Depressed? Terminally ill? "What's gotten into him?" she asked. "I thought Reb would tear up the streets to find the scum who killed Lenny."

Kay turned sideways, putting Lodina's house behind her. Ducking her head, she spoke quietly, as if she thought Lodina might be listening. "He's afraid to find out who did it," she said. "But this is just between you and me."

"Does he have a suspect?" Delia asked eagerly.

Kay shook her head. "I tried to tell him it could be a complete stranger. It has to be, because nobody who knew Lenny would do such a horrible thing. Reb won't listen, though. You know how he is."

"Like a mule." Delia didn't mind Reb's stubbornness; she'd always been able to match it. "He said yesterday that he was worried it would be somebody we know. Are you sure he doesn't have a suspect?"

"Delia, that man could have a harem in his pickup and we'd never know it. But in this case, I think he's making sure *he* doesn't know, either."

Miss Constance wore her favorite pink floral robe with the ruffles at neck and cuffs. "The beauty parlor girl comes every Wednesday," she said, patting her freshly coiffed tresses with her good hand. "Don't cost me a cent, either," she added.

Delia smiled. Not a natural, happy-for-you smile, but a strained grimace that she had always adopted around crazy Constance Winter. Miss Constance had been old when Delia was skipping rope at recess, and all the children had been frightened of the wild-eyed Winter woman. Delia, for one, never outgrew that fear.

Even now, with Miss Constance in her wheelchair, disabled by a stroke and feebled by age, she made Delia nervous. Miss Constance smiled back at her visitor, as if she knew the power she held and thoroughly enjoyed wielding it.

The reigning queen of the Jesus Creek Nursing Home, Miss Constance held court in the lobby. She gave advice to some of the residents, arbitrated disagreements for others, and openly chided the staff when their services fell short of her standards. Everyone in the place deferred to her. And yet Miss Constance Winter was as crazy as she'd ever been, a genetically coded fruitcake just like all her relatives and ancestors.

"Well, you know," Delia said, "Dot Hemby died a while back."

"'Course I knew! She was in the next room from mine right up 'til she croaked. Went in the middle of the night, too, and nobody noticed 'til they started bringing around breakfast. Nobody except me, because I saw the man in the hall."

"The man. . . ?"

"The one who comes for 'em when they die. Snappy dresser, in his way. Always the same one, which surprised me, 'cause I figured Dot would get somebody altogether different, if you know what I mean." Miss Constance gave an exaggerated wink.

Delia hadn't a clue, but she smiled and nodded, hoping to get on with the conversation before the delusions got too murky to navigate. "And afterward, Lenny and Lodina—Dot's children—auctioned off the old Vickers place."

"Figures," Miss Constance snorted. "They're all selling off the family jewels these days."

"But poor Lenny. . . ," Delia paused to think. Was it wise to provide extra details? She decided it was not, then cut to the chase. "Did you ever know Dot's second husband? Pete Vickers?"

Miss Constance gave her a mischievous wink. "He used to pull my pigtails when we was young'uns," she whispered. "And he kissed me once."

Suddenly Delia's grin was genuine as she imagined wrinkled old Miss Constance as a little girl with pigtails! And kissing boys. Had she been loony back then, too? And had Pete known it? "So you could have been Constance Vickers," she said teasingly.

"I reckon if I'd had it in mind, I could've married him," Miss Constance said and patted her hair again. "But I never did hope to be a farmer's wife, and that's all Pete ever was intended for."

So she became a bag lady instead, roaming the town until a stroke took its toll. Delia didn't necessarily consider that a wise choice. "You know, Dot Hemby was Pete's second wife," Delia prodded.

"Oh, they said so, but I can't quite believe it. Mary Gale never would've allowed that. Not that we've discussed it."

"Yes, but Mary Gale was dead by the time Pete married Dot," Delia reminded her.

"All the same," Miss Constance said vaguely, "I don't see Mary Gale taking that for an excuse!"

Fearing that her window of opportunity was closing, Delia rushed ahead before Miss Constance's mind wandered completely down the foggy path. "What about Pete's family?" she asked. "Do you remember anything about them? Did they live hereabouts?"

Miss Constance shook her head and sighed. "They always was peculiar people," she admitted. "Didn't socialize. Pete's daddy—they never did call him by his name, just used initials—seems like he was in the war and was some kind of hero. But after that, he kept to himself a lot. That whole family was like that—rather socialize with hogs than humans."

Delia wasn't sure which war Miss Constance was remembering, but maybe it didn't matter. It was wholly possible that she was making it up as she went along. All the same, she'd take whatever information Miss Constance offered and verify it with more reliable sources later. Delia only hoped she'd learn something to get her started.

"Did Pete have brothers or sisters?" Delia asked. "Any family that might still be alive?"

Miss Constance thought for a minute, then said, "Well, likely none his mama knew about, but sometime when men go off overseas. . . ." She winked again.

For some reason, this made Delia blush, and Miss Constance laughed at her red cheeks.

"No," Miss Constance said. "There's just the boy, and I consider it a shame."

So did Delia, but for entirely selfish reasons. If Pete had siblings, she might find at least one of them alive and coherent. An estimate of dates suggested to her that Pete Vickers might have been the grandson of Jeremiah the schoolmaster, so if he had a brother or sister with a reasonably good memory, she might get lucky. There was no guarantee, of course, that Jeremiah even had offspring or, if he did, that they'd lived in Jesus Creek. Still, tracing ancestry often required educated guesswork as a starting point.

"Miss Constance?" A timid little nurse poked her head around the corner. "It's time for your therapy now. If that's okay?"

The old woman nodded. "In a minute. Just wait there and I'll tell you when I'm ready." Miss Constance returned her attention to Delia. "I guess all your questions about Pete Vickers've got something to do with that body they found out at the Vickers place."

—100—

"Oh, it's just a skull—"

"Would've been a body when it went into the ground, no doubt," Miss Constance insisted.

Delia didn't ask how the news had made its way to the nursing home. It was a fact that Miss Constance knew everything which happened in Jesus Creek. Sometimes people asked her how; Miss Constance said the wind told her. Delia saw no reason to spend time debating the possibility.

"Well, you're right on both counts," she admitted. "I'm trying to learn something about a man named Jeremiah Vickers. He came here in 1878, to teach school." Delia feared that Miss Constance would confess to having been courted by Jeremiah, too, but the old gal was holding her grip on the present.

"Seems to me," she said slowly, "that my daddy went a round or two with a teacher by that name. He used to tell the story of how everybody laughed at this prissy teacher, and I believe the name was Vickers."

Delia's mouth dropped open. "That surely sounds like Jeremiah. Prissy."

Miss Constance gave her a sly glance. "You don't want to fall fool to that one. The others called him prissy, but when this teacher Vickers got into it with Daddy, his daddy—my grandpa Elmer—told Daddy to go back and apologize. He said Vickers oughtn't to be crossed, because he had the Streak."

Delia waited but no explanation came forth. So she asked. "The streak of what?"

"That streak," Miss Constance said impatiently. "The one right down the middle of his face."

There'd been no mention of a birthmark or a physical deformity in Jeremiah's memoirs. Had he found it too embarrassing to mention? Delia reluctantly pushed forward. "I'm sorry, Miss Constance, but I don't know what you mean. Did Jeremiah have a scar on his face?"

For a moment Miss Constance peered into Delia's eyes, as if she expected to find something. At last she said, "I know the rest of 'em are blind to it, but I figured you could see.

No, weren't a scar as such. It's the streak that Satan puts there"—she tapped the bridge of her nose—"to mark his property."

Once again, she'd been taken in by Miss Constance's appearance of sanity. "Oh, in that case I think we're talking about different people," Delia said. "From what I've read, Jeremiah Vickers was a wimp, but a God-fearing one."

"That's what he *was*," Miss Constance agreed. "Daddy said Grandpa Elmer said it just come upon him—the streak on Vickers, I mean. Like as if he'd been taken to the devil in a flash."

Delia looked up at the waiting nurse, who merely shrugged. "Well, I'm keeping you from your therapy. I appreciate your help, Miss Constance."

"You oughta look him up in the newspaper," Miss Constance said. "Pete's daddy was a war hero and you kids don't even care. You ought to take more of an interest in history."

As the nurse wheeled her away, Miss Constance waved good-bye with her good hand and called over her shoulder, "I'll ask Mary Gale how she feels about bigamy!"

Delia wouldn't be at all surprised to learn that Miss Constance played poker with the late Mary Gale Vickers.

She'd hit the library's archive at her first opportunity. And she could hardly wait to tell Roger that his cohort in cosmic curiosity had told her to take a greater interest in history.

Dan McClain's yard was abloom with forensic investigators by the time Delia arrived. Fern Oatley, the state's Forensic Investigator, had already set her team to work. The area around the skull was staked and divided into a giant grid. A young man in jeans and a baggy tee shirt edged his way cautiously around the site with camera in hand while an older man sketched out the scene.

Oatley, though dressed in worn jeans and a Predators tee shirt, was clearly professional. She surveyed every inch of the yard around the skull, taking her time to examine the slightest abnormality in the surrounding soil. Her concentration was so keen she didn't notice the arrival of another spectator.

Delia swore under her breath, annoyed that they'd started without her, and hurried toward the excavation area.

McClain stood on his back porch, intently watching the activity in his yard. Patricia Patrick was at his side, equally intent, but her interest was the living man, rather than the dead one.

"Delia, honey!" Patricia called. "You don't want to get too close. It's positively grim!" Patricia clung to McClain's arm.

At the sound of Patricia's voice, Oatley looked up, saw Delia bearing down on the site, and pointed sternly to the porch before resuming her search. Delia didn't want to alienate the investigator right off the bat; she saw no choice but to join the audience. Maybe she'd be able to sidle away after a brief conversation and join the dig. Just her luck, the woman in charge was a stickler for rules.

"Patricia, I didn't expect you to be here," Delia said truthfully. She took one of the folding chairs McClain had brought outside, scooted it forward for the best view possible, and settled in to watch the show.

"I thought I should," Patricia whispered, as if the confession were a secret. "It's almost sure to be a Vickers, and poor Lodina can't take any more. I'm here in her place, I guess you could say."

McClain glanced at the woman as if she'd spoken a rare Guamian dialect. "Buried without a coffin?" he asked.

"Could be the coffin rotted away," Delia said. "Or I suppose he might've been buried without a coffin at all. Some folks couldn't afford the niceties."

Patricia tightened her grip on McClain's arm. "Oh, that is just dreadful! Imagine poor Lodina living here all those years and never knowing that hideous thing was right under her nose!" She chattered away about the horror of it all, happily oblivious to the lack of attention from Delia and McClain.

Delia quickly decided that watching an excavation was the next best thing to watching someone else play solitaire. From where she sat, her view was often blocked by the investigators, who took excruciating care to remove soil one teaspoonful at a time. Delia imagined the hands of a clock spinning around as the diggers slowly carved out a small trench around the skull.

The process would go much faster if she were in charge; for one thing, she'd order the anal-retentive photographer to click his shutter and move on, instead of trying to create a lasting work of art. "It's possible to be too thorough," Delia complained.

McClain nodded without taking his eyes off the excavation. How, Delia wondered, did he manage to remain fascinated by the process of sifting dirt?

"Why are they going so wide of it?" Patricia whined. "Why don't they just stick a shovel under that awful thing and carry it off?"

"They're digging around the whole skeleton," Delia explained. "Not just the skull. They can't scoop up the skull, dirt and all, because they're looking for itty-bitty bones and bits of bones. And hair, maybe."

Patricia clucked. "We'll be sitting here all day if they don't speed up. How do they even know there's more of it there?"

"Soil discoloration," Delia said. "Body fluid seeps into the surrounding soil as the corpse decomposes."

McClain and Patricia turned to look at her, both of them faintly green around the gills.

"I've got the Discovery Channel," Delia explained.

Eons passed. Species evolved, flourished, and suffered extinction. Still, the forensic team members continued their work. Finally a flurry of activity from the pit caught Delia's eye. "Excuse me," she said to McClain, as she closed the distance between porch and excavation.

Fern Oatley and her team squatted around the shallow hole. Their attention was given to a tiny object in the soil, and they barely noticed that Delia had trespassed. The investigator used a small brush to clean away loose dirt, then gently lifted up the item. Turning it this way and that to catch the sunlight, she squinted, then said, "1954 penny."

Delia fought her instinct to ask questions; she hoped that if she kept her mouth shut, Oatley might not notice her for a few more minutes.

The photographer shook his head. "So do you think the killer's still feeling guilty?"

"Killer?" Delia's vow of silence was broken in response to that word. "You think it was murder?"

Oatley spun around, clearly annoyed to find Delia standing in their midst. For once, Delia's gray hair and crow's-feet paid off; young Ms. Oatley couldn't quite bring herself to be rude to an elderly woman. "Almost certainly," she said. "Looks like somebody may have bashed him in the head."

"Can you tell what sort of weapon?" Delia asked. "Big one? Little one?"

"I could make a guess," Oatley said dryly, "but I'd rather not."

Delia missed the implication and pushed ahead. "The sort of weapon a woman could use? Or would it require more strength?"

The investigator lifted a hand to shade her eyes from the sun. "Who are you?" she asked. "Jessica Fletcher?"

"Delia Cannon." Delia held out her hand, then dropped it again when she realized that Oatley had no intention of responding. "I'm the county historian." It was a harmless fib, she told herself.

McClain had escaped Patricia and the porch to join the gang at the excavation area, and now stood gazing somberly at the earthly remains of the unknown victim. "She might be able to help identify him," he said. "Delia knows everything about this county."

Oatley studied Delia's face for a minute. Finally she said, "This penny was probably in his pocket. It's dated 1954, so the body would have been placed here no earlier than that. Now will you sit down over there and let us get back to work?"

It wasn't much, but Delia felt she'd won a small victory. She trotted back to the porch, pulling McClain along with her. She wanted to speculate, to expound, to theorize. McClain and Patricia, whether they liked it or not, were her audience.

"After 1954," Delia mused. "Pete and Dot Vickers were living here then. Now, Mr. McClain, let me explain that Pete Vickers disappeared one day and never came back."

McClain drew back his shoulders. "So you think. . . ?"

"I think Farmer Pete didn't really go to California to make it big in the movies. I think he ran from a murder charge."

McClain's mouth dropped open, but Delia didn't waste time letting him recover. "The question is, did Dot Vickers know what her husband had done? Or did she really believe he'd been lured away by the glitter of Hollywood?"

"It's such a morbid way to make a living!" Patricia complained, not for the first time. "Don't you know that girl has nightmares?"

An hour after discovery of the penny, the forensics team was still working steadily. Delia nodded, saying "uh-huh" as Patricia rattled on about the horror of murder, bones, and the necessity of uncovering both, while simultaneously weighing the possibility that Dot was an accomplice to murder. Dan McClain, too, was on the porch, but he ignored Patricia's prattle and continued to watch the excavation.

Delia suspected that McClain would be the one to suffer nightmares. He'd been totally silent since the murder diagnosis, never taking his eyes off the work at the excavation site. Either he was the most tenderhearted man on earth, Delia thought, or he regretted purchasing the Vickers farm and was even then concocting a plan to unload the property and its troublesome skeleton.

The young man who'd been scooping away soil and sifting for remains stopped his work. He leaned forward, used his finger to probe the ground, then called over his shoulder to Oatley. The woman didn't hesitate, but dropped her trowel and hurried to inspect the latest discovery.

Delia hit the ground running. Shoving her way into the huddle, she squinted and tried to spot the source of their excitement. "So what exactly is this and what does it tell you?" she asked.

Oatley looked at her with mild exasperation; but blessed

with an abundance of stubbornness herself, the investigator recognized another of her kind. She understood that Delia wasn't going away without answers. "It's a second skull, this one with a nice clean slice in it. Since there's no sign of that injury having healed, it tells me someone whacked this gentleman in the head with a sharp blade shortly before he expired."

"So this second one was murdered, too, but not with the same blunt instrument that killed the first one!" Delia exclaimed.

"Or he committed suicide in a most peculiar fashion," the photographer said dryly.

McClain had released himself from Patricia's grasp and joined Delia at the excavation area. He said nothing in reply to Oatley's comment, merely stood gazing somberly at the earthly remains of yet another murder victim.

"The primary burial is no earlier than '54," Oatley said. "This intrusive one is about two feet deeper. I can't determine a date of death yet, but it looks like we'll have no trouble figuring that out once all the evidence has been examined."

"Several years in between the two, though?" Delia asked.

"Oh, yes," Oatley agreed. "Either a very patient serial killer, or a very popular place for dumping bodies. My money's on the latter."

Clarissa drove with more caution than usual on the way home, as a concession to her sister. Mary remained pale, and her body trembled uncontrollably. "I shall never be rid of it!" she declared more than once. "Every night, when I close my eyes to sleep, poor Mr. Byrd will haunt me."

The others were sympathetic, of course. Jeremiah, in particular, shared her fear that the day's experience would linger, although he suspected—with great shame—that his dreams would be more concerned with his own peril than with the fate of the late Thurston Byrd.

In spite of his eagerness to be on the trail of the robbers, J. D. Howard rode alongside the wagon. Clarissa had urged him once to go on ahead, but Howard—ever the gentleman—

would not leave the ladies unattended so soon after their distressing experience.

They would not be alone, Jeremiah thought with a fair amount of pique, but he said nothing. He could imagine the amused looks on the faces of the others.

Once back at the boardinghouse, Clarissa nearly tumbled from the wagon in her haste to spread the news. She was halfway through the tale by the time the others stepped into the cool of the house.

"Mary!" cried Mrs. Turner when she saw her elder daughter. She leapt from her chair, letting her needlework fall to the floor. "Oh, my child! It's a wonder you aren't dead!"

Mary nodded miserably and burst into sobs upon her mother's shoulder.

"For heaven's sake!" Clarissa crossed her arms over her chest. "You can see she's perfectly safe and healthy. In any case, not even Jesse James is low enough to shoot a woman."

Over her tearful child's shoulder, Mrs. Turner glared at Clarissa. "Shoo!" she hissed. "If you have no Christian sympathy for your poor sister, then get on out and take your wicked tongue with you."

Clarissa flounced out of the room, into the kitchen. Muttered complaints trailed behind her.

"Please excuse me, ladies." Howard eased away from the family tableau. "I must gather a few things and be on my way."

Mrs. Turner, still consoling Mary, barely acknowledged his departure.

Jeremiah fell into step, following Howard through the wide doorway into the kitchen. He did not consciously form a plan, and yet his pride, so recently maligned, was already puffed up and ready to explode.

Clarissa sliced a bread loaf as if it were the bandit Jesse James himself. She looked up as the men entered, her expression grim, lips set. "Oh, Mr. Howard," she said. "I've bundled up a few bites for you to take along."

"That's right kind of you, Miss Clarissa." Howard flashed her a grateful smile.

"Ahem." Jeremiah, even though his voice trembled, was determined to speak. "If you've no objection, Mr. Howard, I'll go along with you."

Both Clarissa and Howard stood silent, as if their ears had abandoned them. At last Howard spoke. "Ride with me back to town, you mean?"

Jeremiah shook his head. "I mean to follow along with the posse."

Once again his audience found that speech eluded them. At least, Jeremiah thought gratefully, they didn't laugh outright.

At last Clarissa put down her bread knife, wiped her hands on her apron, and, in a most unexpected turn, appealed to his logic. "But Mr. Vickers, you have no horse."

Such an obvious complication! And such a face-saving way out of his braggart's foolish promise. But if he were to give way so easily, he would seem a buffoon as well as a coward. "I expect I could borrow a mount," he suggested.

Howard stood silently by, letting Jeremiah navigate the maze alone.

"Mr. Vickers," Clarissa sighed, as if she couldn't understand why he ignored the obvious objection to his proposal. "All we have to offer is Mad Jack. He's old and fat and ornery." She was kindhearted and did not mention Jeremiah's great fear of horses.

Jeremiah accepted with relief his fantasies of heroism for what they were, and knew that he had made an even greater fool of himself by pretending he had the courage or the skill to ride with the posse, with the *men*. He turned away quickly to hide the final indignity—hot tears which sprang to his eyes.

"Just this morning," Howard said suddenly, "I purchased a fine mare. She's kept at the stable in town. If you'd care to ride her, Mr. Vickers, I would enjoy your company along the way."

Jeremiah looked to him, half-expecting Howard and Clarissa to burst into peals of laughter, not sure whether Howard was sincere. "I wouldn't want to impede your pursuit of the scoundrels," he said. Dared he pray that Howard would agree?

"There's more to tracking than speed," Howard said. "If your mind is set on it, we'll be on our way."

Jeremiah swallowed hard. "Then I'll gather a few things," he said and stepped toward his destiny.

While the men bundled a few necessities for their adventure, Clarissa sliced extra bread to pack with smoked meat. At the last minute she pulled four fried apple pies—intended for that night's supper—from where they cooled, wrapped them in a cloth, and added them to the sack.

She had her misgivings, of course. But there was so little chance that Mr. Vickers and Mr. Howard would catch up to the posse—let alone to the outlaws!—there seemed no reason for concern.

Miss Clarissa Turner, let it be noted, would have made a poor living as a prophetess.

CHAPTER TEN

THE INVESTIGATOR AND HER SMALL TEAM had worked steadily through the day, giving up only when dusk made careful examination of the site impossible. The work may have been routine for them, but their attention to detail was astounding. Delia tried every ploy in her repertoire, but Fern Oatley remained steadfast; no civilians would be allowed on the dig. No more relaxed rules, no questions, no answers, and—most of all—no interruptions of the team's work.

Fortunately, Delia thought, *she can't run me off the porch without Dan McClain's help.*

Delia detected relief on McClain's face when Patricia finally returned to town. "Lodina needs me with her," Patricia explained, "when she views . . . Lenny."

Clearly more interested in skeletons than in romance, McClain barely acknowledged Patricia's departure. At first he'd been stunned by the second discovery—more so than by the first—but as artifacts continued to reveal themselves, his shock turned to deep interest.

By the end of the day, Oatley had taken pity on the dedicated watchers. As the team closed up shop for the day, the forensic investigator cast a wary eye toward the two, shook her head as if arguing with herself, then strode across the yard toward Dan McClain's back porch.

"Okay, Mrs. Fletcher." Oatley propped one foot on the bottom step and looked squarely at Delia. "I don't want you dying of curiosity because, with my luck, I'd be charged and convicted of your murder."

Delia saw no reason to hold a grudge, especially when she was about to get most of what she wanted. "So what can you tell me? Us, I mean."

From the corner of her eye, Delia saw Dan McClain lean forward as if he, too, had a question. Even Fern Oatley waited for him to ask, but McClain remained silent.

"We have two reasonably well-preserved skeletons," Oatley began. "Not perfect and not complete, but I've got enough bits and pieces to start."

"They were both murdered?" Delia asked. "You're certain of that?"

"They both suffered head injuries that could have—and probably did—kill them. Neither injury shows signs of healing. I'm reasonably certain they were both murdered, yes."

Delia nodded. "But don't you find it peculiar that there are two bodies buried several years apart, and one on top of the other?"

"Peculiar?" Oatley shrugged. "Like I said, out back of the barn is a handy place to put a body."

"But it wasn't very deep, that first grave," Delia pointed out.

Oatley raised a questioning eyebrow. "You ever tried to dig a six-foot hole in Tennessee clay?"

Delia had, in fact, once planned a lovely rose bed in her front yard. She'd barely been able to get the shovel to break the soil and, within ten minutes, had decided she could be perfectly content with an imaginary flower bed.

"The penny gives us the earliest possible date for that one burial," Oatley went on. "And a few other artifacts in the same strata narrow the date of the burial a bit more. Probably before 1963."

"The man who once owned this property," Delia put in, "ran off, left his wife and children, and was never heard from again. It may have been that he left during that time period. I can find out."

Oatley didn't jump at the offer of assistance. "What makes you think that's not him out there?" she asked.

"That never occurred to me," Delia admitted.

"You mean it could be Pete Vickers in the grave?" McClain asked. "Can you prove it?"

"We'll certainly try to identify the remains," Oatley said.

"Whoever it is. That's part of the job."

"DNA would help," Delia said, "but Pete doesn't have any relatives. At least, none around here. I've been looking into his ancestry, though, and—"

"Wonderful!" Oatley was genuinely enthusiastic about this offer. "Why don't you make that a priority? It would be very helpful for DNA testing."

Delia understood that she was not being encouraged to continue her genealogical research in the interest of science. Rather, Oatley viewed this as a way to get rid of a meddlesome old bat. She didn't mind—not a lot, anyway—because it was a way in which she could contribute to the investigation.

"But what about the second skeleton?" McClain asked.

"The second skeleton is in worse shape, but there are lots of artifacts preserved along with it." Oatley actually allowed herself a smile. "Sometime between 1877 and 1880, he was dumped into the outhouse."

Delia hated driving at night. February's gloomy days seemed to last forever, but in fact they disintegrated into darkness before 6:00 P.M. and it was nearly 7:00 by the time Fern Oatley's team packed up their equipment.

Roger was making lasagna at his apartment, and Delia was sorely tempted to go straight there. Unfortunately, her sense of propriety insisted on at least a quick trip to the funeral home first.

She'd change into dress clothes and throw some jeans in the car, Delia decided as she pulled into her driveway. A few minutes of consoling remarks with the other mourners would have to serve; she was starving!

Grabbing her purse from the car seat, Delia jogged across her leaf-littered yard. Her back porch spanned the width of her house. It was hidden from view of the street and, therefore, a perfect storage area for all the odds and ends she picked up at garage sales. One day, Delia vowed, she would sort through the items, but for now they constituted a veritable maze.

She was negotiating her way through the narrow path to

her back door when she heard the *bang*. At first Delia thought the wooden floor had cracked and given way beneath the weight of her treasures. The sound came again, and this time she recognized it for what it was—a gunshot—just as her body collapsed.

Delia thought it odd that she was fully alert and yet felt no pain. She had no idea what time it was, but she estimated that she'd been unconscious for no more than a few minutes.

Assessing her situation, she determined that her body was wedged between a dilapidated steamer trunk and a wringer washer. The first order of business, she concluded, was to free herself before the shooter tried again. Unfortunately, neither her arms nor her legs obeyed the command.

"This is a fine mess," she mumbled. How was she supposed to call 911 for help if she couldn't even stand up?

The man on the steamer trunk sighed. "It's the way of things," he said sadly. He was thin—*cadaverous* sprang to mind, but Delia assumed that was because she'd spent so much time around skeletons lately—and she was certain she'd never seen him before.

"I'm Delia Cannon," she said. "And you are. . . ?"

"Jeremiah Vickers." He bowed slightly from the waist, and for the first time Delia noticed he was standing inside the trunk.

"Now this is a wild coincidence," she said, "because I've been trying to track you down. In fact, I was just at your house earlier tonight, right before someone took a shot at me."

"There's a shameful lack of courtesy these days." Jeremiah shook his head. "You appear to have suffered more than a passing injury. I expect you'll find the condition worse if help doesn't arrive soon."

Delia chuckled. "'Tis not so deep as a well, nor so wide as a church door, but ask for me tomorrow. . . .'" She could feel blood sliding down her face and realized she hadn't just fallen; she'd been shot! "Am I dead?" she asked as a matter of curiosity.

"Not yet," Jeremiah told her.

"In that case, I'll make good use of this opportunity." Delia closed her eyes but found the image of Jeremiah was still sharp. "I'd just gotten to the part of your memoirs where you joined up with the posse."

"A poor choice it was," Jeremiah admitted. "Pride drove the wagon."

Delia wasn't surprised to hear this. Everyone but Jeremiah knew he had no business riding off after criminals. "If you don't mind talking about it, I'd like to hear the tale. I have a bad habit of getting caught up in other people's lives."

Jeremiah was silent for so long that Delia opened her eyes to see if he'd left. He was still there, gazing into darkness, maybe reliving the adventure.

"Well, at least tell me if the bank robbers were ever caught," she insisted.

Mr. Howard's advice to me was simple: Just give the mare—Medusa, by name—her slack, and let her follow Red Fox.

"Will we go east, or follow the sheriff to the river?" I asked.

Mr. Howard swung himself easily into the saddle, his movements and seat as comfortable as if he walked upon solid ground. For a timid farmer, J. D. Howard on horseback more closely resembled a centaur.

He looked up and down the main street, squinting as if that would help the decision. "Neither," he said. "We'll head south."

"But—" I began.

Mr. Howard's horse stepped out and, as predicted, Medusa followed closely on his heels. The horse's jerky movement threw me off balance and I instinctively grabbed for the saddle horn.

"The robbers went in separate directions," Mr. Howard said, "but only one side has the money. They have to meet somewhere to divide it up."

It was plain sense, I realized, and yet I questioned. "You think? But the sheriff didn't—"

"The sheriff had a hot trail and he may well catch up before the gang doubles back. All the same, we'll head south, toward the Natchez Trace."

I was still befuddled. "Why do you think the outlaws will meet to the south and not the north?"

Mr. Howard turned in his saddle, even as his horse moved into an easy lope. Grinning at me, he said, "I had to pick one direction or the other, and I've not much mind to go north again."

I could sense there was a jest in this, but the meaning eluded me.

With a more serious expression, Mr. Howard added, "The Trace is a good place when you're on the owl hoot. Even if the bandits run up against other riders, it'll more likely than not be their own kind. And they think they've gotten away clean; they won't be on the alert."

At the end of town, where the main street divided, Mr. Howard nudged his animal off the road and began to follow a narrow path into the woods. Negotiating the ditch with dread, my heart rose up into my throat. Good sense was enough to tell me that this was a fool's quest for honor. Foreboding descended upon me, even before I cast a longing glance back toward Jesus Creek; there, I saw the madman Elmer Winter watching intently, his mouth moving soundlessly.

I couldn't help but wonder whether he blessed us or cursed us.

Once into the woodlands, Mr. Howard paused only long enough to call out, "Hold on tight, Mr. Vickers. We're in for a ride now!"

I have no idea how long the torture lasted, but my body believed it to be a dozen hours at the least. Surely the ride could not have lasted so long, for the contrary sun barely moved overhead.

My horse kept pace with Red Fox, who alternately trotted and galloped. Unable to match the rhythm, I was tossed up and down, side to side, without a moment in between to catch my breath or restore my balance.

After the first few minutes of paralyzing terror, I gave my life into the Lord's hands. Pitching forward, I wrapped my arms tightly around Medusa's muscled neck, closed my eyes, and prayed that my death would be quick. There was no possibility it would be dignified, not with my backside high in the air.

"The posse has likely turned back," Mr. Howard shouted, "but the robbers will have it just as bad!"

I barely heard him over the steady roar of rain. The storm had broken loose when we'd been on the trail an hour; lightning and thunder terrorized the horses, and the clay soil—now mud—sucked at their hooves, causing numerous stumbles. At least, I thought, the conditions caused Mr. Howard to slow his pace, although his concern was for the horses and not the schoolteacher.

It was near dusk when Mr. Howard brought his horse to a stop and Medusa followed suit. "May as well stop for the night," he said, sliding to the ground.

The horses seemed almost as grateful as I felt. At first the soaking rain had been a welcome relief, bringing respite from the heat and dust; then it began to drip incessantly down my collar, my shoes squished, and I couldn't see—not that I had opened my eyes for more than a few minutes in total.

Mr. Howard removed the saddle from Red Fox and tied the animal to a tree at the creek's edge. He turned to find me still astride Medusa. "Trouble, Mr. Vickers?" he called.

I was shamed again. "My legs," I told him. "They don't move."

This admission brought only a quick gleam to Mr. Howard's eye. "Remove your feet from the stirrups," he suggested, "and leave your legs to hang. You'll find the condition improves shortly."

I did as instructed while Mr. Howard rummaged the clearing for any dry twigs hidden beneath the brush. By the time a tiny campfire was burning, I felt stinging pain in my lower limbs. Joints creaking, I lowered myself to the ground and nearly collapsed; my legs were still weak as a baby's and protested every movement.

"Give you a hand with that saddle?" Mr. Howard offered, even before I'd made an attempt.

"I'll give no pretense. My strength is gone; and in any case,

—117—

I don't know which piece of the contraption to untangle first."
I stumbled away from the mare and collapsed against the
base of a broad tree.

In no time, and with little effort, Mr. Howard removed the
saddle from Medusa and led her to the creek as companion
for Red Fox. As soon as this chore was completed, he joined
me by the weakling campfire and held out a bundle of food.

Huddled beneath the tree, I found that sitting on the
flooded ground was no more comfortable than being in the
saddle. Unlike Mr. Howard, who paced to stretch his legs, I
couldn't stand; my legs quivered still, and I feared the cramp-
ing would never go away.

"Miss Clarissa's thoughtfulness," Mr. Howard said as he
unwrapped his bread, "will save us. A bit to eat, Vickers,
and you'll be a new man."

"Then bury the old one now," I said, "for he's useless to
you in the chase."

Mr. Howard chewed his share of the meat thoughtfully.
"You'll ache a bit, I reckon, but it'll fade. Takes time in the
saddle to make a horseman."

I had already made my vow to keep both feet planted
firmly on the ground if I lived to walk again. I picked bite-
sized morsels of chicken from the bone and pondered the
possibility that this promise might never be kept, should we
encounter the killers. Perhaps I would not live to return to
Jesus Creek and face the derision that awaited me.

Mr. Howard leaned back against the broad-trunked oak,
pulled up his collar, and closed his eyes, as if enjoying a fine
spring day. I watched him enviously. I have never learned
how a man disregards the woes that encircle him, to find
even a moment of peace amid the maelstrom.

"You know, Vickers," Mr. Howard said, "come morning,
you could head on back to town. The sheriff and his men
will have given up the chase once the tracks washed out. You
might let 'em know I've headed this way. Send them in to
assist, in the event I catch up to the robbers."

I considered the suggestion, fondly imagining the comforts
awaiting me at Mrs. Turner's boardinghouse. If I could only

get back onto Medusa, I'd head for home immediately. Except. . . "I don't know where I am. How can I find my way back through this sodden jungle?"

"Just let the horse lead the way," Mr. Howard suggested. "She'll get you there."

I weighed the options available: continue on the trail for as many days and nights as it took to find the outlaws, possibly coming face-to-face again with the notorious killer Jesse James; or return alone through the dark trails of the Natchez Trace, where I could, if I chose, walk instead of ride the demon animal.

"Is that your recommendation?" I asked. "That I return to town?"

Mr. Howard opened one eye and assessed me. "Never easy, is it? To make a decision that, ultimately, shapes our character. What is the right, when all factors are considered? And which path do we take, when the world says one direction is best, but our hearts and minds and neighbors declare that we should travel in another?"

"We're gentlemen," I reminded him. "Our talents and skills are better suited to a more civilized place than this frontier. In another society, in more propitious circumstances, we could choose easily enough."

Mr. Howard pulled a worn and battered Bible from his vest pocket. "I find this always comforts me," he said, "whenever I begin to doubt my choices." Laying open the book, Mr. Howard recited the words printed there. I say *recited* because I could not have read it in the dim light from the fire; he, with his weak eyes, must have been nearly blind in the night.

Therefore is my spirit overwhelmed within me; my heart within me is desolate.

I remember the days of old; I meditate on all thy works; I muse on the work of thy hands.

I stretch forth my hands unto thee: my soul thirsteth after thee, as a thirsty land.

Deliver me, O Lord, from mine enemies: I flee unto thee to hide me.

With food in my stomach and soothing words upon which

to, indeed, meditate, I found my circumstances more bearable. Mr. Howard and I enjoyed a companionable silence as we gazed at the dying embers. The morning would be soon enough to decide my course.

We had ridden through the morning and covered a good bit of ground. "For your sake," Mr. Howard said to me, "I wish we could take it slower, but the robbers will ride hard and we're already at a disadvantage."

"Never mind," I said to him. "I find the going easier now." I was not ashamed of the lie, for I knew it to be the path any man of good standing would take. The truth of it was this: my limbs were chafed to the quick by constant contact with the horse, my spine believed it had been struck by hot daggers, and whole portions of my anatomy vowed revenge for the punishment inflicted on them. And still I clung to Medusa's mane, praying all the while that I had not compounded one mistake with a greater error.

At last Mr. Howard held up one gloved hand, signaling a halt. "I'll just stretch my legs in the woods," he said. "If you'll hold the horses now, I'll return the favor."

We both dismounted—he with more grace and speed—and I took the reins of both horses. Our time together had worked a miraculous change in Medusa; the mare had grown attached to me and now began to press her nose against my sleeve. My clothes were already beyond repair, and I confess the affection she showed me was flattering. For this reason, I allowed the blasted female to rub her forehead against my arm.

This proved to be an unfortunate misunderstanding. With her exquisite strength, Medusa succeeded in shoving me off my weary legs. In a flash, I was on the ground, scrambling about on all fours in an effort to avoid being trampled. In the process I had let go the reins, and both Red Fox and the fickle Medusa ran off into the woods where Mr. Howard had disappeared. I am certain the two animals snickered as they went.

For that moment I put aside concern about the unnecessary delay caused by my incompetence. I chose instead to wallow in the pure joy of stillness. From my position, I allowed myself to stretch full length upon the muddy ground. I basked in the luxury. Bliss is found in simple things.

At first I paid no heed to the sound of branch and brush being crushed underfoot, for I expected Mr. Howard to return. I raised my head to humbly accept whatever abuse he heaped upon me for loosing the horses. Thereupon I saw not one but two men, leading their horses behind them. Both looked down at me across the length of their gun barrels.

The sight of them turned my mouth to cotton. Before—in the bank—I'd seen only the cold hard eyes above the outlaws' kerchiefs. Those same merciless eyes stared back at me now.

"Well, well. The fancy gent." Jesse James grinned, and a cold chill went through me. "If you'd told me you wanted to die, I'd've obliged you back at the bank."

The killer trained his gun on me, playing with his prey. I, unarmed and horizontal, had no recourse. I closed my eyes and began to pray, a child's prayer of protection which came instinctively into my mind.

The sound of a single shot jolted me, and my prayer stopped mid-sentence. Opening my eyes and raising a hand to my face, I felt for the blood that surely must be streaming forth from my face. Or my neck, or from my torso. I continued to search for the fatal wound, even as I saw the outlaws, one now unarmed and nursing his wrist, staring slack-jawed at a point behind my vision.

At first I thought ghostly spirits were afoot, playing their pranks in the dark misty trails of the Trace. For only a second, though, was I so deluded, and then a voice came up from behind me.

"Pulling a gun on an unarmed man?" Mr. Howard asked. "Where's the challenge in that?"

Jesse James stared dumbly at his empty hand, then at me, and finally his gaze moved to Mr. Howard. His open mouth dropped wider, then spread into a ghoulish grin. "Why, Dingus, you're a sight for sore eyes," he said. "Are you playing nursemaid to this fop?"

In reply, Mr. Howard fired two shots in rapid succession, one neatly taking down the second gunman, who dropped to his knees, whining and mewling like a motherless kitten. He dragged himself behind a tree, pulling the reins of his horse with him. In a flash of movement, he was astride the beast and galloping away from us, through the wooded trails of the Natchez Trace. The second shot, as accurately fired, had pierced the heart of Jesse James.

I, still on the ground, found it impossible to turn my face away from the hideous sight. The outlaw's body collapsed, section by section, until the corpse lay facedown in the mud, reminiscent of my own position. His toothy grin remained until the last.

Mr. Howard walked the few steps across the glade and held out a hand to me. Frozen in shock, I didn't know whether to accept or decline the aid.

"He was going for his other gun," Mr. Howard said matter-of-factly. "I'll collect our mounts. You take the grain sack from that saddle there." He pointed to the outlaw's horse which still lingered in the clearing, tranquilly chewing at grass tufts.

Once these tasks were accomplished, Mr. Howard helped me to mount Medusa. Then he collected the money sack from me and attached it securely to his own saddle. "It's the best we can do for Byrd," he said, "to return the bank's money."

"Shouldn't we. . . ," I jerked my head toward the body, "take care of matters?"

With a disinterested glance, Mr. Howard said, "Leave him for the buzzards, as he'd have left you."

Our horses stepped away, followed by the horse belonging to the dead outlaw, and we moved along the trail at a steady lope. We had accomplished our aim and now headed for home, with considerably less exhilaration than I had imagined in my heroic fantasies.

It was not a Christian thought, but all the same, I was glad that the devil Jesse James was dead.

CHAPTER ELEVEN

DELIA WAS DISAPPOINTED when she woke and immediately recognized the sickening smell of the Medical Center's antiseptic halls. The cramped room was too small to be her own, so she immediately deduced that she was still in Emergency Treatment.

She considered saying it anyway—*Where am I?*—but knew Roger would rib her mercilessly for her lack of creativity. Instead she opted for what she hoped was a feisty line: "The license plate number was NCC-1701."

Roger was hovering at her bedside when she opened her eyes and got them focused. "I'm right here," he said, gripping her hand.

"Of course you are." Delia's voice was weak, but she had her wits about her. If she'd given it any thought at all, she'd have assumed Roger would be by her side at all times. "Where else would you be?"

"Doc James is lining up a private room for you right now," Roger explained. "You should've been conscious when you weren't; he used some colorful language to describe your injuries. For that matter, I'm none too pleased about the lasagna sitting cold and lonely in my kitchen."

"How did I get here?" Delia asked. That was surely a logical question, and not entirely cliche.

"I came looking for you, of course," Roger explained. "When you didn't show up for food, I knew something was amiss. I mean, when's the last time you passed up my legendary zucchini lasagna with garlic bread? I figured you were at the Vickers place, enthralled by that skeleton, but I spotted your car in the driveway when I went past your house."

Movement at the foot of the examining table caught Delia's eye. "Is that Reb? Or am I hallucinating?"

"While we're waiting on the room," Reb said, "I thought I'd ask a few questions about . . . the incident."

"The incident?" Delia asked. "When somebody takes a shot at me, I use a stronger word than *incident*." Closing her eyes eased the pain a little. Still, Delia would have traded all her worldly goods at that moment for a hearty dose of Demerol.

Shouldn't there be a hole in her memory? She'd read somewhere that head trauma often causes a loss in short-term memory, wiping out the events that immediately preceded the cause of the injury. And she was absolutely certain she'd suffered head trauma. "Somebody tried to kill me." Speaking quietly made no difference—her head continued to pound out a rap rhythm.

Roger's grip tightened. "Do you know who it was?" His voice was low. And intense.

For the first time, Delia realized fully what had happened to her. "Oh! Do you think it was personal?" she asked. "Or just a hunter with bad aim?"

"Now, Delia," Reb said soothingly, "why would anyone want to hurt you?"

With her free hand, Delia reached up to inspect her aching head. A gauzy bandage was taped to her forehead, and she suspected her skin color was in the purple range, but otherwise. . . .

Roger leaned over the treatment table and gently kissed the top of her head. "You owe me ten years."

"Sorry. Won't let it happen again." She shifted slightly and felt searing pain run up her left leg. "Oh, no. Did I break something?"

"A couple of china pieces you bought at that junk store last summer—"

"Something on me?" she explained.

"Only your head," Roger told her. "The bullet grazed you, but you clobbered your noggin pretty good when you fell. And you've twisted your ankle, but that's minor. Dr. James says you'll be walking the streets in no time."

"Probably have to," Delia said, "to pay his bill."

"I'll start the questions now," Reb said, "while you're still in a spunky mood, because your good humor won't last long. They aren't going to give you anything for pain until you've been cleared on that head injury."

Delia tried to groan but produced only a whimper. "Ask. Then shoot me."

It didn't take long to establish that Delia's memory of the attack was useless. She hadn't seen the shooter, hadn't noticed anything out of the ordinary when she'd pulled into her driveway. "Well, doggone it," she protested. "It was dark and I wasn't taking notes."

Reb and Roger both seemed exasperated with her lack of details, but what could she do? She wasn't in the habit of searching her yard for homicidal maniacs every time she came home.

"Can you at least tell me whether the shot came from the back or the side of your property?" Reb was persistent.

"I told you. It was dark. I was minding my own business when I heard the shots, and then I was unconscious." The boys weren't the only ones losing patience.

Delia wanted painkiller, and she wanted it immediately. "If anything comes back to me," she promised, "I'll tell you right away. I'm on your side, remember? Now will somebody get me a Tylenol and a discharge, please? I've got work to do."

Reb gave Roger a hearty backslap. "Told you she'd be her old self in no time. You worry way too much. And now that my work here is done, I'll get back to little matters—like skeletons in the backyard and finding whoever killed Lenny Hemby."

A small wave of guilt washed over Delia. "I'd forgotten all about Lenny," she admitted. "Any progress?"

"None," Reb confessed. "I'm hoping for a miracle."

Roger gripped Delia's hand a little tighter, and he gave the police chief a stern and challenging look. "You don't think that's related to what happened to Dee, do you?"

After a moment's thought, Reb gave Delia a steely look and asked, "You haven't been snooping around, have you? Playing at investigator?"

Delia shook her head a fraction of an inch to either side. "Cross my heart. I've been so involved in the skeletons, I haven't had time to think about Lenny. Besides, all I know about that is that somebody broke in and shot the poor guy. I wouldn't know where to start snooping."

Reb remained skeptical. "You haven't been asking questions? Encouraging 'innocent' conversations about Lenny?"

"Really and truly," Delia insisted. "You know, Reb, it's not like I want to get involved in crime. I can't help taking an interest, though, when it lands in my lap. In fact, the forensic investigator asked for my help."

Roger and Reb affected the same skeptical expression.

"Really," Delia insisted. "Have you heard there are two skeletons? The first one was buried in the late '50s or early '60s. Reb, do you know when Pete Vickers was last seen?"

"Who?" Reb asked.

It was a stellar moment for Roger. For the first time since he'd lived in Jesus Creek, he took center stage with his recitation. "Pete Vickers was Dot's husband, but not Lenny and Lodina's father, because Dot was his second wife after Mary Gale, who died young."

Reb took a moment to process Roger's convoluted tale. Then, with a heavy sigh, he said, "You've gone over to the dark side, Roger. I thought you were immune, but I should've known you'd crumble under Delia's evil influence."

"It took years of effort, but I'm quite proud of my handiwork." Delia cast an approving smile in Roger's direction. "And Pete disappeared. Roger, honey, would you like to tell the story?"

"You go right ahead, my love." Roger stepped back to allow her the stage.

Because she knew Reb loathed extraneous detail, and because talking recharged her headache, Delia told the story as succinctly as she could. "And naturally it occurred to me," she finished, "that Pete might have killed somebody and run away to avoid prosecution. The other most likely possibility is that Pete is the skeleton."

"Either way," Reb said, "you'd think Dot would have mentioned it."

"Maybe she didn't know," Delia suggested. "The body was buried behind the old barn. Suppose the grave was covered with some heavy piece of farm equipment, something there'd be no reason to move. An old tractor tire or a pile of lumber—whatever leftover parts people might save for no particular reason. Dot probably never knew the grave was there."

"But she knew her husband succumbed to the lure of California," Roger reminded her. "Where did she get that story?"

"Either from Pete as he dashed out the door, suitcase in hand and dripping blood," Delia offered, "or from Pete's killer, who needed to cover his tracks."

Reb shook his head to show he disagreed. "If I told you Roger had moved to California—he didn't even bother to say good-bye—and you never heard from him again, would you blindly accept that?"

"Of course not," Delia said. "But maybe Dot wasn't overly bothered by Pete's absence. If the marriage was in trouble, for instance, his sudden disappearance worked to her advantage. She got rid of a husband with no fuss or bother."

Reb took a step closer to the door. "I guess you're gonna pick at this mystery for a while."

"You bet," Delia promised. "One way or another, I'm going to find Pete's family. DNA, you know. I just might solve the case."

"What about the other skeleton?" Roger asked. "You said there were two."

"That's a toughie," Delia admitted. "Now, Roger, don't make a tasteless remark when I tell you this. Try to remember the man died a tragic death." She paused for a moment before explaining, "The second body was disposed of in an outhouse."

Reb snickered. "That gives new meaning to—"

"Hush!" Delia said. "I didn't think I'd have to warn you. Can't either of you boys behave?"

"Okay, I'll be good," Reb promised. "And I'll make you a deal. You work on the mystery of the skeletons and let the TBI take care of Lenny's killer. Doesn't that sound like an organized, efficient way to proceed?"

Roger raised his hand like a schoolboy. "And who will track down the sorry scumbag who tried to kill Delia? Because, quite frankly, that is the only case I care about solving."

"Don't worry, buddy," Reb said as he exited the room, "I've taken a personal interest in that one, myself. See y'all later."

As soon as Reb's steps faded away down the corridor, Roger leaned over and kissed Delia's cheek. "Tell me something," he whispered in her ear. "Is that the truth? About you not snooping around?"

"Why does everyone accuse me of that?" Delia demanded. "One time I happened to find a dead body. It's not as if I go looking! It's not as if I run around with a magnifying glass and a gun."

"Shhh." Roger put a finger gently to her lips. "I was just checking. Sometimes—now, you know it's the truth, Dee—sometimes you start imagining that you can solve any mystery, genealogical or otherwise."

"I like puzzles. I like to untangle twisted thread and bring order to chaos. That doesn't mean I fancy myself a sleuth."

She tried again to rearrange herself for a more comfortable position, moving much slower and more carefully this time. "But I certainly don't go looking for deranged killers. You know me, Roger. I'm a big ol' scaredy-cat. I don't clean house because I have a paralyzing fear of dust bunnies."

Roger had to admit that his domestically challenged significant other had made her point. "The truth is, Dee, I don't believe you'd do anything deliberately stupid. It's just that you start picking at that knot, trying to untangle it, to soothe your own curiosity, and all of a sudden, you're the target of a killer."

Roger turned pale and reached again for her hand. "I don't care," he said, barely audible, "if the jerk had a stroke and accidentally pulled the trigger as he passed over to the other side. As soon as he's found, I aim to put a Diamond Cutter on him."

The normal clanks, squeaks, and moans of the hospital were suddenly overridden by Dr. Daryl James's booming bass. Delia heard him greet the orderly outside her door, comment on the weather, and ask for a gurney to be brought to the ER treatment room right away.

"Roger, listen," she said. "There's something I want you to do for me."

"Anything, my love," he promised.

"Go to my house and bring back that manuscript, the one I bought at the auction."

"Honey, do you really think you'll feel like reading tonight?" Roger asked.

Delia wiggled her finger, beckoning him to come closer. "Roger," she said. "I do have something to tell you. There was someone on my porch."

"Did you see who it was?" he asked.

"Of course. We had a long talk before you got there."

Roger sighed heavily. "This is another one of those Delia moments, isn't it?"

"Huh?"

"You had a long conversation with the person who shot you. Only you, Dee. Only you."

She held on tightly to his hand, tugging him toward her. "No. I had a long talk with Jeremiah Vickers. The dead guy. I heard his story about riding with the posse. You think I'm crazy?"

"My dear, I've known it all along. Why else would you be with me?"

Delia gave him a tiny, cautious smile. "I got the story from his own lips. If that's not documentation, I don't know what is."

Dr. James burst in then, not bothering to lower his voice. Giving Roger a quick thumbs-up, the doctor referred to Delia's chart, noting the most recent set of vital signs before asking Delia how she felt.

"Dandy!" she told him. Her perkiness would have made Kathie Lee seem lethargic by comparison. "Just a teensy headache, but otherwise I'm rarin' to go."

"You lie like a dog," Dr. James said. "But it's superficial aches and pains. Between your good habits and normally excellent health, plus a dose of unnaturally good luck, you've come through this adventure in pretty fair shape."

"I'm glad to hear that," Delia said. "May I please have some aspirin now?"

"No," the doctor said cheerfully. He rolled the still-loose pages of her emergency room records into a cylinder and used it to tap out "Shave and a Haircut" on the end of the treatment table. "But maybe I'll send some home with you tomorrow. Provided you don't turn up any disturbing symptoms during the night and that you eat the green Jell-O."

The worst of it was scooting from treatment table to gurney, then from gurney to hospital bed. All that shuffling set off a new series of pain that found its way into every inch of Delia's battered body.

Once she was settled in her own room, though, with the promise of peace and privacy in the near future, Delia began to organize. "Roger, I'd really appreciate it if you'd run to the house now and bring back those memoirs. It looks like a bunch of loose pages, inside a box on the coffee table. Oh, and treat it with extreme care, please."

"Delia." Roger's voice was unexpectedly firm. "Maybe you should leave those memoirs alone for a while. Until your head clears up, at least."

The young nurse fussing with Delia's bed sheets disagreed. "Won't hurt her to read," she said. "And besides, she'll need something to keep her busy all night, 'cause we're sure not gonna let her sleep!"

"You're not?" Delia asked. "I thought rest was always prescribed for hospital patients."

"Oh, it is," the nurse agreed. She took the call button from its place on the wall and pinned it to Delia's pillow. "But we're gonna wake you up every hour to ask if you're in a coma or just sleeping." Satisfied that her patient was as comfortable as circumstances allowed, the nurse added, "You wanna have some fun? Just don't respond at all when they check on you about one o'clock. The midnight shift never gets much excitement." She exited with a chuckle.

"Your offspring?" Delia asked Roger as the nurse's rubber soles squeaked away.

"I'd be proud to claim her," he said. "Now let's get back to the memoirs. I think you've spent too much time with dead people lately. Why not take a break from it?"

"Because I want to find out if what's written in the memoirs matches what Jeremiah told me," Delia explained.

Roger frowned, stepped closer to the bed, and looked into her eyes. "Delia, you do know it was a dream. Jeremiah's ghost didn't appear to you."

"Excuse me?" she said tartly. She didn't mean to be short with him, hadn't realized she was annoyed until the words were out of her mouth. It felt good to vent her frustration, though, so she went with the flow. "I suppose instead of a ghost, it might've been an extraterrestrial Jeremiah clone."

"That's not the same thing," Roger said defensively. "Don't get upset. I'm just trying to—"

"I'm not upset. Tell me why it isn't the same thing," she challenged.

"Look, why don't we come back to this topic tomorrow?" Roger suggested. "After you've had some rest and you're thinking clearly again."

"Fine advice from a man who roams the woods in search of alien poop!" There was little Delia enjoyed more than winning an argument, but this one was such an easy battle, it hardly felt like victory.

"I don't go out and get the poop myself," he countered. "I send—"

"You send the logic-challenged out to do it for you. Now," Delia said, with reasonable calm, "why don't you bring me Jeremiah's memoirs? If the written tale of the posse ride doesn't match the story I heard from Jeremiah, you can say you told me so." She watched with deep and full satisfaction as Roger surrendered and headed out to do her bidding.

By raising the head of her bed a few inches and keeping her eyes closed, Delia had reduced the throbbing headache to a pulsating pang. Her ankle didn't care what she did; it continued to torture her.

The major contributor to her foul mood, however, was the

undeniable gap in the narrative. She'd refused to look at it while Roger was present; to be perverse (in Delia's opinion), he'd insisted on remaining by her side for a full hour after he'd returned.

When at last he'd kissed her good night and left the building, Delia grabbed the memoirs from the bedside table and shuffled recklessly through the pages, searching for the section that recounted Jeremiah's adventure in the clearing.

It was missing.

She'd refused to believe it at first, but a thorough search through the pages of the manuscript drew an oath loud enough to bring a nurse running to check on Delia's condition.

Jeremiah's carefully numbered pages crushed all her hopes of convincing Roger and of learning the truth for herself. The entire section where the posse ride should have been chronicled was simply not there.

Almost as disturbing was the discovery that several other sections of the memoirs were also missing. Who knew what other vital pieces of information were lost forever?

"I knew you'd be grumpy after the shock wore off." Dr. James popped through the door, on his way home after a long day. He pulled the visitor's chair away from the wall, seated himself in it, and propped his feet on Delia's lowered bed rails.

"You have no idea how grumpy," she warned him. "How long do I have to suffer before you give me drugs?"

"All through the night," he told her. "But I can bring you an aromatherapy candle, if you want."

Delia did not find his humor endearing. "Lenny's funeral is tomorrow," she reminded him. "I have to be out of here in time to attend."

"Nope," the doctor said. "You can have somebody videotape the service, if you really want to see it. But you won't be there."

"Oh, puh-leese!" She was no longer trying to hold her temper in check. "What difference does it make whether I go home in the morning or the afternoon?"

"Delia, tell me the truth." Dr. James pulled a pipe from

his shirt pocket and pointed the stem at her. "Are you in any kind of shape to walk down the hall? Do you honestly believe you could sit through a funeral service? Or do you think maybe you should be still for a few days and let your body heal?"

She refused to give him the satisfaction of an honest answer.

In the long dark night of her medical incarceration, Delia Cannon was surprised by the resurgence of a skill she'd thought was lost forever.

"It was just like when my daughter was a baby," she explained to the nurse who brought her breakfast. "I halfway woke up long enough to tell them I was okay, then went right back to sleep."

A night's rest coupled with oatmeal, toast, and pulp-free orange juice restored her spirits; and even her pummeled body felt workable, if not strong and agile. Delia chose to ignore her behavior toward Roger and Dr. James. *Why ruin a good day with guilt?* she reasoned.

She'd just finished breakfast and was contemplating the odds of obtaining a chocolate chaser when Roger arrived. He poked his head around the door and assessed her mood before committing himself to full entry.

"Hi, hon!" Delia blew a kiss across the room. "Got a Hershey Bar on you?"

Thus encouraged, Roger bravely crossed the room and presented her with a box of chocolate-covered cherries. "I'm psychic," he said. "I knew you'd want chocolate."

"Roger, sweetie, it doesn't take much of a psychic to figure that one." Delia ripped into the box and shoved a candy into her mouth. "There's not a thing in the memoirs about what Jeremiah told me. We both lose."

"I prefer to say we both win." Roger sat on the edge of her bed, careful not to jiggle her injured leg. "Are you drugged? I like it."

"Not yet." Delia reached for another chocolate. "But Doc promised to give me the good stuff today. Now if I can just convince him to let me out of here in time for Lenny's funeral."

Taking his life in his hands, Roger helped himself to a chocolate-covered cherry. "If you love me, you'll forget about that. Then I'll have an excuse for skipping the funeral myself."

"Knock, knock!" Patricia Patrick popped into the room, carrying a plate of chocolate-chip cookies covered with tinted plastic wrap and tied up with ribbon. "I'm glad you're awake!" she said. "Didn't want to bother you, but this is the only free time I've got today. I'll just put these cookies on the night-stand, and if you aren't allowed to eat them, you can always send them home with Roger."

Patricia was the most *morning* morning person Delia had ever met. The nervous energy that drove Patricia to chatter, clean, and create ceaselessly was equal to that produced by the Big Bang.

"I've got to get on over to Lodina's," she went on. "She'll need somebody with her today."

Delia jumped in as soon as Patricia stopped for breath. "Thanks so much for the cookies, Patricia. It's sweet of you to come by, too. Do you think Lodina will understand if Roger and I don't make it to the funeral?"

"Oh, Delia! There's just no way you could be there, not after your awful accident. It's a miracle you're alive."

"If you would, Patricia," Roger said, "let Lodina know how sorry we are to miss the service."

"I'll tell her," Patricia promised. "Of course, she barely knows what's going on around her. She went all to pieces yesterday, right there over the casket. We couldn't calm her down, so Frankie Mae and I finally just put her in the car and drove her home. Even then, I had to give her one of my nerve pills to get her quiet."

Patricia takes nerve pills? Delia thought. She nearly dropped her chocolate while trying to imagine what Patricia would be like without them.

"And then this morning," Patricia exclaimed, "I heard the Vickers place had burned to the ground. I tell you, there's a curse on that house!"

CHAPTER TWELVE

Memoirs of Jeremiah Vickers, chapter 24, page 437

I recall little of our return beyond the blessed numbing of my limbs and seat. The events of the day conspired, with wicked irony, to remove the senses that allowed me to recognize the discomfort of my circumstances.

Mr. Howard, once again resuming his gentle demeanor, led us at a brisk pace toward Jesus Creek. So far as I could see, he was not affected by his actions in the glade. That is to say, there was no outward expression of regret or fear. I knew, however, that the man who had, only the night before, comforted my spirit with his profound choice of verses from the Holy Book could not help but be affected by our harrowing encounter. He was not inclined, to my relief, to discuss the matter.

As for myself, I am ashamed to say that I held no pity for the late Jesse James. From this day, I lamented, I shall never be able to represent myself as a man of charitable conscience. Still, I could muster no sympathy for the dead outlaw. I fought to keep his evil face from intruding upon my thoughts, preferring to remember his corpse lying facedown upon the cold ground.

Lest the reader think me mad—generously assuming that the horrible sight of Mr. Byrd's cold-blooded murder, followed by the close proximity of my own death, unhinged my mind—I state here in my own hand: I enjoyed the vision of the dead man. I took comfort in the knowledge that he posed no further threat to innocent men. I was comforted to know that his flesh would rot and be consumed by feral beasts in the eerie forest of the Natchez Trace.

Mr. Howard and I camped another night on the trail, but this time there was no talk of the wisdom in Scripture. We spoke little, aside from the necessary passing of information. We ate the remains of bread and meat, washed down with fresh water from a spring which flowed near our campsite. And when these mundane chores had been tended to, we slept. If Mr. Howard suffered from any fright in the night, I was not aware of it. As for myself, I slept soundly, without dreams.

As fortune would have it, our return to town was met by Elmer Winter, who may have stood guard during our absence, for he remained upon the very spot where I had last seen him. Spying our approach, his whiskered face split into a ghoulish grin. "You be the stragglers!" he called to us. "Sheriff and 'em give up the chase and gone home."

Mr. Howard waited until we pulled our horses abreast of the drunkard to reply, "Find the sheriff and tell him we've brought back what was taken."

Winter's grin quickly turned to slack-jawed amazement. "You got back the money?" He did not wait for a response, but spun on his heel and scurried down the street and into Delia's Tavern to spread the news.

Taking advantage of the moment, I eased my sore and aching frame to the ground, only half-daring to believe that I was well and truly rid of the beast Medusa. So severe were my injuries, I recall the pain—the agony!—even as I write these lines, though it be many years later. To know that my feet need not leave the ground again until my final farewell was nearly as incomprehensible as the memory of recent events.

Immediately those about on the street, having overheard Mr. Howard's instructions to the drunkard, surrounded us. They were soon joined by a crowd which swarmed forth from the saloon. I tried but could not isolate a single voice from the buzz.

Mr. Howard proceeded as if he were alone on the street, removing himself from the saddle and leading Red Fox to a nearby trough. I followed suit, having been reminded that Medusa, too, had earned her rest.

As we stood there, too worn and weary to concern ourselves with the citizenry, Sheriff Leach pushed his way through the crowd to greet us. His expression was quizzical. No doubt he distrusted the ramblings of Elmer Winter, as any sensible man would do. "We lost the trail in the storm," he said. "Stinger's men, too. Old Winter says you fared better." He tried on a questioning smile.

For answer, Mr. Howard reached up and released the grain sack from his saddle. Without a word, he handed it over to the stunned sheriff.

I cared not for the gasps and cheers around us, nor for the worshipful glances directed at J. D. Howard. My only desire was a hot bath and a feather bed. Mr. Howard, though, maintained his stamina and proved himself once again. "Mr. Vickers and I had better luck," he explained. "He drew their attention, allowing me opportunity to retrieve the bank's money."

Put in those words, the tale made me out to be an equal to Mr. Howard. I could see disbelief on the faces of the sheriff and those around him. I have lost my compassion, I told myself, but not my honor, and I attempted to set right the story. "In truth, only Mr. Howard—" I got no further before the gentleman stopped me.

"I tell you," Mr. Howard said to them all, "this schoolteacher is built of stronger stuff than we allowed. Without his nimble mind and quick action, the bank would not have its money." He took my hand in his own and shook it firmly.

From the corner of my eye, I saw that Elmer Winter had witnessed this speech with skepticism. He looked directly at me, smirked, and spat.

Word of our return preceded us to the boardinghouse. Mrs. Turner and her daughters waited on the front porch to welcome us home. At the sight of us, Mrs. Turner clasped her hands to her bosom and cried out, "There they are, our brave heroes!"

On her right, Miss Mary Turner raised a hand to shield her eyes from the setting sun. On the left, Miss Clarissa looked us over carefully. When she had assured herself that we bore no life-threatening injuries, the impetuous young woman lifted her skirts, leaped from porch to ground, and raced across the yard to meet us.

"Clarissa!" her mother cried, horrified by the girl's behavior.

Miss Clarissa paid her no mind. She first threw her arms around me, unaffected by my disgraceful appearance and offensive odor, then offered the same warm greeting to Mr. Howard. "Oh, I'm so proud to know you both!" she exclaimed. "Your courage! Your steadfastness!"

She went on in this fashion until both Mr. Howard and I were as rosy-faced as blushing schoolgirls. At last, even Mrs. Turner grew tired of the effusive (although sincere and well-intentioned) praise.

"Give our gentlemen room to breathe, Clarissa!" she commanded. "Let's all go inside, away from the heat. There'll be time for thanks after supper."

Miss Clarissa insisted on leading both horses to the barn. I noted with envy how firmly she handled the pair, then remembered that I had survived the trek atop wild Medusa. Perhaps I might ride again one day, I thought. In the far distant future.

The ladies of the house prepared a hot bath, and Mr. Howard graciously insisted that I take the first turn. Regular bathing, though necessary and desirable, cannot compare to the pleasure of a much-needed washing after strenuous exercise. I was tempted to indulge myself until the water had gone cold, but eagerness to speak bluntly with Mr. Howard spurred my actions. Before I could have a word with the gentleman, however, there were more pressing matters to attend to. I dressed in fresh clothes and combed my hair while Mr. Howard took his turn at the tub.

The hot water having somewhat soothed my aching bones, I found that I was inexplicably inclined to stroll about in the settling dusk for a bit, realizing only later that it was nerves that made me move from spot to spot instead of resting. I had walked the boundaries of the property a full three times before we were called to the table.

Despite the usual rigid adherence to schedule, on this night Mrs. Turner insisted on preparing a meal for "the men who saved the bank." She soon had created an enormous feast, and I ate heartily while Mr. Howard related our tale to the ladies.

Miss Clarissa listened attentively, interrupting only once to ask for further explanation. Her sister, less enthralled, picked at her food and gave no sign that the narrative held her interest.

Mr. Howard's edited description of our confrontation with the outlaws brought a gasp to Mrs. Turner's lips and ended her elder daughter's meal altogether. For a moment, it appeared that Miss Turner might swoon, but an iron grip on her arm—administered by Miss Clarissa—halted such intentions.

Thus restored, Miss Turner turned her head away from the conversation and sulked. Miss Clarissa clapped her hands and asked for more details.

Once the tale had been told, and much of it told again, I thanked Mrs. Turner for the fine supper and invited Mr. Howard to join me for fresh air.

"Go on," Mrs. Turner encouraged us. "Take a stroll and talk the way men do. I'll clear up the remains, but should you find room for another plate of cobbler, you'll have it served at any time."

We made our departure, and when Mr. Howard suggested we sit for a while on the back porch, I urged him to continue on to the barn. "I have sat enough" was my excuse, but in truth I wanted to assure that we would not be overheard by the ladies.

As soon as we were well removed from the house and its wide open windows, I at last broached the subject that troubled me. "You were kind to include me as a partner in your story." I said this outright, for I was truly grateful for his gesture and did not wish him to take my next statement as a criticism. "But," I went on, "you have stretched the truth so far, it may snap."

"What is it you mean?" he asked. "Have I mistold it, Mr. Vickers?"

He would continue the pretênse, I realized, until I forced honesty from him. "I was neither your partner nor your companion," I reminded him. "With no thought for you or the objective, I went along to make myself seem something I am not."

The late summer was evident in the still-warm air of the night. Back there, beyond sight of the house, the grass grew tall, and weeds plucked at our legs as we passed.

There was, of course, a clear path to the privies just beyond, but otherwise the yard behind the barn was unkempt. Excess items and tools no longer in use were stacked and piled there. This disorderly state surprised me, for Mrs. Turner kept her house in such a state of high shine and polish that my dear mother would have been hard put to fault her housekeeping skills. They were of a kind, those two women, and neither ate the bread of idleness.

I reminded myself that these, though, were farming tools. No doubt they'd last been employed by the late Mr. Turner and were beyond the strength and scope of Mrs. Turner and her daughters. I felt the master of the house, having been the sole user of such objects, must be blamed for their disarray.

As we passed behind the barn, Mr. Howard halted his steps and glanced sharply at me. "What is it you think you are not, Mr. Vickers?"

As if he needed to be told!

"One thing I am not is a horseman." I could smile now as I admitted it.

Mr. Howard smiled, too. "I've known men—and women, for that matter—who handle a horse with more assurance. But aside from that, you managed the most important part; you stayed in the saddle."

This, of course, was not the topic I wished to pursue with him, and I chose to argue the matter no further. "As for my 'distraction' of the outlaws," I said, harking back to his earlier words on the street, "I surely did not provide such."

"You surely did!" Mr. Howard argued. "The gunmen had

two targets, feet apart, one high, one low. Had you been at my side, they'd have picked us off clean. So you see, Mr. Vickers, you did draw their attention, long enough for me to shoot."

It was a deceptively simple depiction, one that could easily fool an audience who had not witnessed the scene. I knew that Mr. Howard's version of it had been concocted for just that purpose. Designed to improve my standing in the community (for what reason, I could not say), his telling did not resort to untruth; it merely rearranged words to imply a truth that never existed.

Perhaps Mr. Howard's intention was to convince me of my value in the circumstances. He had known me but a little while and was likely unaware of my clear notions about my own substance.

"I was no threat to them," I said. "I possessed no weapon, and in any case, they had already ascertained my character in the bank. Had you given them the chance, both outlaws would have fired their guns at you and then killed me or not, as they saw fit."

"But they could not have known you were unarmed," he argued. "Dared they take the chance? Could they be sure which of us was the faster draw?"

"One look at me—"

"Tell me, Vickers: why do you refuse to accept your appointment? You're a hero."

"I had no intention of being a hero," I pointed out. "I merely stumbled and was too tired and frightened to get to my feet."

The moon's light struck his eyes and caused them to glow, blue as a morning sky. "Heroes never recognize their acts, do they?" he asked. "A man who rides out after killers without fear shows no more bravery than a dog chasing a squirrel. Real courage, Mr. Vickers, is facing that which we fear. The minute you put yourself on Medusa and rode into the woods, you proved your courage."

I knew that, in another's case, this might be true. His logic was flawless. But I felt no pride in my actions, for I knew my motive had been vain and shallow, not the pure inspiration of a champion.

There was no point in continuing the case. Mr. Howard, as true a gentleman as I have met to this day, would continue to represent me as a hero. It was my responsibility to live with what I knew to be the truth of it, and no concern of his.

I turned to walk away but was stopped by the sound of a familiar voice. "Well, Dingus, you leave an easy trail behind you."

The same fear which had churned my belly for days returned. I wanted to run, to hide inside Mrs. Turner's comfortable house. I most certainly did not want to turn and look at the speaker, the escaped outlaw and partner of Jesse James.

My body, of its own accord, spun around, and there I saw the robber. He stood between the gentlemen's and the ladies' privies, his gun pointed directly at Mr. Howard. I concluded that he had waited behind the structure for a convenient moment before confronting us.

"Jack Ladd," said Mr. Howard. His voice was steel, his shoulders firm. There was no fear in J. D. Howard, only a calm acceptance of his fate.

The bandit wore a blood-soaked bandage around his lower leg, where Mr. Howard's bullet had entered. So he had, indeed, escaped, but not into the anonymous woods of the Trace. Instead, he had followed us here. I had no doubt that he meant to demand return of the treasure he'd stolen, and which was now returned to its rightful owner.

The three of us formed a triangle, with the bandit cleverly positioned so that he could face both Mr. Howard and myself. It was an easy thing for him to swing his gun from one of us to the other, but of course, he kept it mostly focused on Mr. Howard. "I don't suppose you'd want to share your taking," the bandit said, with a grin. "You're not a sharin' man, are you?"

Mr. Howard remained calm, his voice steady even in the circumstances. "The money has been returned to the sheriff, Jack. If you want to avoid a noose—or the fate of your friend, Vaughn—you'll head out of here now."

It was clear to me that Mr. Howard and the outlaw were acquainted. I merely noted this unexpected revelation, without exploring it at the time. Nor did I question the identity of Vaughn or his fate. There were more pressing matters to assimilate, and I gave my full and cloudless attention to those.

"Money's not what I come here for," the bandit said. "It's revenge, pure and easy. I mean to have it, for myself and Vaughn, and the reward that'll go with it."

What reward he meant, I could not fathom, unless he yearned to spend his eternity in Hell. All the same, I could see that his sights were set on violence. Surely he would kill us both, and—a horrific thought occurred to me for the first time!—afterward perpetrate crimes against the ladies of the house.

"Have you forgotten the old days?" Jack Ladd continued talking, even though Mr. Howard gave him no encouragement to do so. "Did it slip your mind what the banks and the law set out to do? Or has preachin' got into you so deep, you've turned saintly?"

"I tell you again," Mr. Howard repeated, "take your life while you have it and get out."

Jack Ladd was unimpressed by the threat. "I don't see sign of losing my life anytime soon. You're a good shot, but you ain't the fastest, and my gun's already drawed. You'd be dead before the ground felt you. I daresay your partner there won't be of much help to you in a fight, either."

The outlaw looked at me with scorn plainly displayed on his face, but his gun did not waver. He kept it pointed at Mr. Howard's head, perhaps more concerned by the gentleman's serene behavior than by his threats or his gun.

At that moment, I heard Miss Clarissa call out from the house. "Mr. Howard! Mr. Vickers! Are you out there? May I have a word, please?"

The outlaw's eyes darted from Mr. Howard's face to my own. "Lucky I keep enough bullets to take care of myself," he said. "Somethin' I learned from an old commander. Didn't you, Dingus?"

I never knew I possessed the grace and speed necessary, and yet I managed the task! In one movement and without conscious thought or concern for the consequences, I grabbed up a rusty ax which leaned against the back of the privy and, without thought or aim, swung it in the direction of the bandit.

He must have seen the movement, quick though it was, for he began to turn his gun upon me. Before he could fire, the ax blade, strengthened by momentum, knocked the legs from under the injured man. As soon as he fell, I swung again, this time placing the ax firmly in the middle of his head. Jack Ladd's skull split neatly open before his sneer disappeared.

For the third time, I watched as a man slipped into death, his eyes barely registering the fact. Each time, it seemed to me, I felt less care for the victim. I have told myself repeatedly in the years since, that in the latter cases, the dead were killers themselves, who would surely have been sentenced by a court to the same fate as repayment for their crimes.

There was a moment of stillness in which it seemed to me that the world stopped spinning, the frogs stopped croaking, and the night air ceased its course across the landscape. Both Mr. Howard and I stared down at the lifeless body of the villain, stunned to realize that our dangerous predicament was ended.

"Mr. Vickers," Mr. Howard said quietly, "I believe I owe you my life."

At that very moment, Miss Clarissa bounded around the corner and greeted us breathlessly. "There you are!" she cried. "I was hoping you might come inside now. I have more questions about—"

Mr. Howard grabbed her in his arms and turned her away from the horrific sight that waited upon the ground. "Look away, Miss Clarissa," he instructed. "There's no need for you to witness what has happened."

True to her nature, Miss Clarissa immediately broke from his grasp and stubbornly turned back to examine the corpse which lay in her own backyard. "I'm very glad it isn't daylight," she said, "because if I saw it clearly, that would cause me to faint like Mary."

Despite her bold words, the lady appeared somewhat unsteady, and so I repeated Mr. Howard's advice. "Please, Miss Clarissa," I begged. "Return to the house. Mr. Howard and I will tend to this."

"Tend to it?" A laugh caught in her throat. "What is it, may I ask? No, no. I can see what it is. I meant to ask, how did it come about? And why here? What has gone on since you gentlemen stepped out for fresh air?"

Mr. Howard turned to me, helpless against the curiosity of woman. "We may as well tell the story, Vickers, as it's clear that Miss Clarissa will not leave it be. But surely she'll not want to distress her mother and sister by retelling such a disturbing episode. Isn't that right, Miss Clarissa?"

The lady nodded firmly. "Oh, certainly, sir. I can keep a secret. I often do. But you must enlighten me—does that wood splitter in Mr. Vickers's hand figure prominently in the story?"

I was stunned to realize that I still held the weapon with which I had dispatched the villainous Jack Ladd. Instantly I dropped it to the ground, then fell to my knees and attempted to clean the sticky blade with soil and grass from the yard. Like Lady MacBeth, I seemed unable to stop scrubbing until at last Mr. Howard knelt down beside me and pulled my hands away from the weapon.

"Enough of that for now," he said. "Brush off your hands and let's get on with what needs doing."

And so we were compelled to explain that the corpse upon the ground was, in fact, the outlaw Jack Ladd. We detailed his escape from the glade and explained to a breathless Clarissa Turner that he had tracked us back to Jesus Creek and was on the verge of committing murder against Mr. Howard and possibly myself.

We discretely omitted mention of what might have become of Miss Clarissa and her family, although I am sure she was clever enough to foresee the possible outcome, had Jack Ladd lived.

"Vickers is the hero again," Mr. Howard ended. "But now we must dispose of the result."

"We might call the sheriff," Miss Clarissa mused, "but that would require that my mother and sister learn the details of your night's work. I believe it would be best for them to remain ignorant."

Neither Mr. Howard nor I commented, but we agreed, quite naturally.

"After all," Miss Clarissa went on, "this man is a vicious killer, or at least, he condoned the murder of Mr. Byrd. Best for all that he is put to rest along with his doomed soul."

"It may be," Mr. Howard said thoughtfully, "that his soul has found the only peace an outlaw may hope for—in the grave."

"If you'll go on about your business, ma'am," I told her, "Mr. Howard and I will dig a grave for him where it'll not bother you again."

"That would take half the night!" Miss Clarissa protested. "If I may make a suggestion? There is one place on the property where neither my mother nor my sister—nor I, for that matter—would likely step foot. A place built, in fact, for disposal of dung."

Many have complained that I am lacking in humor, but Miss Clarissa's pun did not elude me. In spite of my shock at her use of the vulgar word, and even though I disapproved of such derogatory reference to any human being, whether good or evil, I could not help but be amused. It was some time then, before we were able to proceed with Miss Clarissa's quick-witted plan. When my laughter was at last under control, I found that my jaw was added to the list of body parts that ached.

CHAPTER THIRTEEN

"IT'S THE PERFECT OPPORTUNITY for you to get acquainted with your Christmas gift!" Roger said gleefully. "I'll teach you to use the computer tonight."

Within minutes of her official release from the Medical Center, Delia was struggling to dress herself in the tiny bathroom. This procedure was made more complicated by the fact that Roger had brought her fresh clothes, and he'd chosen her skinny-day jeans (she definitely was not having a skinny day) and a turtleneck sweater that had shrunk to the size of a tea cozy. Delia distinctly remembered having shoved the darned thing into the back of her closet years before; only Roger could have managed to pull it out without noticing all the perfectly suitable and properly sized clothes that hid it from view.

Uncomfortable as she was, Delia decided against asking him to bring her another set of clothing. That would only slow down her escape.

"Reb came by while you were gone," she called to Roger. "He says the Vickers place is a complete loss. The old place was just kindling waiting for a lit match."

She emerged from the bathroom, carefully maneuvering through the doorway on her new crutches. "Mr. McClain came through the emergency room about three o'clock this morning. I haven't been able to talk to him yet, but one of the nurses told me he's going to be fine. He sucked in some smoke, but otherwise—"

"Too much coincidence, I'd say." Roger's normally cheerful expression was nowhere to be seen. "Someone took a shot at you, then tried to kill McClain. All this happened just hours after you two dug up a couple of skeletons. . . . It's all tied together."

Delia nodded. "More than coincidence, surely. But what could either of the dead men have to do with us? And what about—oh!"

Roger leapt to his feet. "What is it? Are you dizzy? Hurt? What?"

"No, I'm fine." Delia waved him away irritably. "I just realized, though—Patricia was there with us. Yesterday, during the excavation. We should warn her that she could be in danger."

"Oh, right." Roger laughed out loud. "Like there's a killer on this earth who would tackle Patricia. Besides, she was fine this morning. If she made it through last night, she must be out of the woods."

"Or the would-be killer stopped for a burger before going after the third member of our group." Delia hobbled across the room and picked up the phone. "I'll be ready in a minute. I just want to let Patricia know what's up."

Once back at Delia's house, Roger had carried her from the car into the house and gently deposited her in the bedroom. The first order of business, then, was to change out of her clown costume and into a warm sweat suit and thick socks.

While she dressed, Roger set about moving half the furniture she owned to accommodate her needs. His concern and devotion created an overwhelming sense of guilt, and so Delia reluctantly agreed to his demands. "But only a very short lesson," she said. "I'm still weak."

Thus encouraged, Roger dragged in a chaise lounge from the yard and fitted it out with blankets and pillows, so that Delia could recline in relative comfort beside the dining room table. This left almost no space between the sink and the table, but Roger insisted on proceeding. It seemed like a great deal more trouble than it would be worth to Delia, but it was far preferable to Roger's alternate suggestion—moving the computer into the middle of her living room.

As soon as Delia was stretched full length beside the blasted contraption, Roger fired up the computer and began babbling instructions at her. He was enjoying himself so much, in fact, that he didn't notice when Delia took a few moments to nap; she was eager for sleep, vaguely hoping that Jeremiah's ghost would appear in a dream to tell her she hadn't been dreaming the first time.

"Delia!" Roger's voice jerked her awake.

"Sorry," she said. "What was that last thing you were just doing?"

"I said," he repeated, "that I've activated your e-mail account. Henceforth, you shall be known as Delia@JesusCreek.com. Now this is your password." He scribbled a series of numbers and letters on a Post-it note and stuck it above the monitor. "Memorize it. Share it with no one."

"But you already know it," Delia said.

"I don't count. Okay, pay attention here. To open your e-mail, double click on this icon—the one that looks like. . . ."

As Roger droned on about the many options available to her (and just why would she need to use multicolored text, Delia wondered), his words blurred to a gentle, rhythmic white noise. Delia closed her eyes and drifted into slumber once again.

"Delia, wake up." Roger nudged her arm. "Wake up. You're missing the most important part. I was explaining about search engines," he said, with only a trace of pout in his voice.

"Gasoline or electric engine?" she asked, hoping he wouldn't notice she'd completely lost the thread of the conversation.

"Search engine. When you want to find something specific on the Internet, you use a search engine. Just type in a few key words about the subject you're interested in, and you'll see a list of Web pages about that subject. Now everybody has preferences, so you'll have to experiment to find the search engine you like best."

"I'll do that," Delia promised.

"I've written down the URLs of some of the best ones, and they're taped to the monitor. I've bookmarked them, too, and you should always remember to bookmark any site you like."

"Okey dokey," Delia agreed cheerfully.

"So let's try it." Roger's hands were poised above the keyboard. "What shall we search for?"

"I dunno," Delia said. "What are the choices? And what do we win if we find it?"

Roger glared. "This isn't a game. It's a useful tool. You're always at the library or the state archives, digging through dusty old books. The Internet is much more efficient—"

"Yes, Roger, but those are birth and death records, marriage records, baptisms, and census records. Important documents," she pointed out.

Roger nodded. "And you can find them right here, from the comfort of your own living room."

Delia bolted upright, allowing the twinge in her foot to sneak past the painkiller for just an instant. "You mean there are genealogical records in that thing? Why didn't you say so in the first place? Help me into a chair and show me which button to push!"

Two hours later, Delia considered herself an Internet expert. She had mastered the art of Search (but was still iffy on the concept of Right Click) and had successfully bookmarked three very promising Web sites devoted to genealogy.

Roger had been relegated to the chaise when Delia took over the command center, and now he sprawled among the pillows. His attempts to retake the computer had met with dismal failure in the face of Delia's fierce search for land grants and census records. "I don't know why this surprises me," he said.

She ignored his caustic remark. "Does Jesus Creek have a Web site?"

"Yes," he replied wearily. "It's www.JesusCreek.com. Just type in—"

"You know," Delia went on, "we could put all the county historical records on it, and—oh, shoot!"

"What?" Roger leapt to his feet in hopes that she'd accidentally erased the hard drive or downloaded a virus. Any disaster would do, just so long as he would be called upon to fix it.

"I should be looking for Jeremiah!" Delia quickly typed in the name, then clicked SEARCH. "Would you look at that!" she said with awe in her voice. "This'll keep me busy for days!"

Roger sighed and rose from the sofa. "I'm going to make coffee."

The tone of his voice finally penetrated Delia's cyber-drunk brain. "Honey, look," she said, actually turning away from the keyboard to give her full attention to Roger. "You don't have to stay here, sweetie. Why don't you go home and play with your own computer?"

"And leave you alone? You just got out of the hospital!" he protested.

"But I feel fine. And I'm only going to sit here looking at Web pages for a while, then I'm going to bed. What are you going to do? Watch me snore?"

Roger couldn't argue her point, but he was clearly reluctant to leave her to her own devices. "What if you need something? What if you fall, or some new symptom appears? What if you accidentally kill the computer?"

"I have this handy high-tech gadget called a telephone," she reminded him. "And I know how to use it. Or maybe I'll just send you an e-mail."

This promise made Roger deliriously happy. "Great idea!" he said. "I'll go home and send you an e-mail, then you can practice sending one back to me. Maybe after that, we'll do a real-time chat."

"One thing at a time, dear," Delia begged. "I don't want to overload myself."

She barely noticed when he left. With the introduction of Search Engine into her life, Delia felt as if she'd been given access to the Akashic Records. All sorts of topics came tumbling out of her brain, each one demanding to be investigated immediately.

"This Internet thing is incredible!" She was talking to herself, of course, but she didn't feel alone. Not with all those like-minded souls right there, only a click away. Thousands of ancestor trees—some of them jazzed up with animated art—waited for her to find them. Delia was part of a great big virtual family!

She was suddenly grateful for the accident that had her stuck at home. It gave her a perfect excuse for sitting in front of the computer, surfing the Net, and possibly finding a hundred new clues in the ongoing mysteries of genealogy.

Using one of the search engines Roger had shown her, Delia typed in the name *Jeremiah Vickers*. Instantly a dozen Web sites were listed. Delia was elated, but after checking out all twelve sites, she realized that none of them furthered her pursuit of the elusive schoolteacher; every single site was devoted to the ancestry of Jeremiah's mother's line, but not one offered more than a name and estimated birth date for Jeremiah.

That information might be helpful later on, but for now Delia wanted more plot and fewer details. How, she wondered, could she narrow the search terms? She grabbed a sheet of paper and scribbled possible words and phrases, using anything she could remember from the memoirs.

She saw no reason to search for such a common name as *Mary Turner*; there were bound to be thousands of those. "Almost as bad as William Smith," she grumbled. Honestly! Why didn't people try to give their children unique names?

There was no point in looking up the families she was already familiar with. Leaches, Wilsons, and Winters were fully documented in the library's genealogy section. Some of the more ambitious members of the Historical Society had gone beyond pedigree charts and had written detailed accounts of their ancestors' lives, then presented bound copies to the library.

"Outlaws!" Delia was surprised it hadn't occurred to her sooner. Surely there was a Web page about bank robberies. She might even find a reference to the heroic deeds of Jeremiah Vickers and J. D. Howard. Why not start by looking for an account of their deadly encounter with Jesse James?

Delia tried another one of the search engines on Roger's list. "LibraryHQ.com," she muttered and squinted at the scribbled note. "Click on—what is that? Site Source."

She ought to insist that, if she had to learn to use a computer, Roger had to learn to write the old-fashioned way—with legible penmanship. On the other hand, once she'd deciphered his notes and discovered that Library HQ held a wealth of fascinating documents, she forgot her complaints about his scrawl. There were dozens upon dozens of old books, journals, and diaries that she'd waste no time in getting back to, but for now she was only concerned with Jesse James.

The first Web site she found was devoted to the James-Younger Gang, and it produced disturbing information: Jesse Woodson James had died on 3 April 1882—not in the late summer of 1878—and in St. Joseph, Missouri, rather than on the Natchez Trace in Tennessee.

"Now what's that all about?" Delia wondered aloud. "And who did Mr. Howard shoot if not Jesse James?" She clicked on link after link, hoping to find an explanation for the discrepancy, but all accounts gave the same information as the first.

There were even a few sites devoted to the premise that Jesse James had faked his death, changed his name, and lived to a ripe old age, producing a multitude of children along the way. While Delia was not sufficiently educated on this subject to form an opinion, she did find it intriguing. With an eye toward further investigation at another time, she bookmarked the most promising pages.

Was it possible that Jeremiah had confused the story, or possibly taken liberties with the characters in his tale in order to make the bank robbery seem more exciting? There wasn't a single item to suggest that Jesse James had died in Tennessee.

Scrolling as she pondered, a sentence suddenly leapt off the screen: *J. D. Howard was an alias used by Jesse James at various times throughout his career.*

Delia laughed out loud. "Well, butter my butt and call me a biscuit!"

It took her a few minutes to find her e-mail screen, and several more to translate the menu and narrow down the options. In time, though, she managed to fire off her very first e-mail. Appropriately, it went to the man who had brought both romance and cyberspace into her life, and it contained a single sentence, typed in all caps: *I LOVE THE INTERNET!*

Memoirs of Jeremiah Vickers, chapter 34, page 512

I shall never forget the day I learned the truth of the matter. My students were reciting their multiples, so it must have been near the hour of 11 A.M. Suddenly the schoolroom door burst open, and there stood my wife, slightly disheveled as always, but radiant in her blessed condition.

I had known that she would be in town to collect a few household items, but certainly I had not expected to see her before I returned home for the day. This unexpected visit brought immediate fear and trembling, for she would not interrupt my work unless a tragedy of the highest order had occurred.

Instructing the children to continue their lesson, I hurried to the door and gently pulled Miss Clarissa outside. Speaking quickly and quietly so that the pupils would not hear, I asked her plainly, "What is it, my dear? What has happened?"

A tear welled in her eye. "Jeremiah, you'll never believe it. They've killed Jesse James."

For a moment, I naturally thought that her delicate condition had affected her mind. "Jesse James has long been dead," I reminded her. "Four years now, in spite of the many bogus claims of imposters."

Miss Clarissa shook her head, loosening a curl in the process. "No, Jeremiah. This is the real one, and it's true for a fact. The word has just come to Sheriff Leach, and everyone is talking about it. I don't want to be the one to tell you, but who else could do it? Oh, Jeremiah. It's our good friend Mr. Howard. He was the outlaw Jesse James, and now he's murdered. Shot in the back by some dirty little coward!"

The frustration was overwhelming! How, Delia wondered, can there be so many references that are useless? She was ready to throw in the towel when a glimmer of hope flashed on her screen.

The ancestor tree for Pete Vickers was skimpy and obviously

of no interest to the person who'd compiled it. Still. . . . "Peter Vickers, born circa 1910 in Tennessee!" It was the closest Delia had come so far. She realized it might refer to any Pete Vickers in any part of the state, but she was optimistic.

This particular Peter Vickers was the son of J. D. Vickers, born circa 1882, also in Tennessee. Hadn't Miss Constance told her that Pete's father was known by his initials? The Web site was loaded with information about J. D.'s in-laws—clearly the focus of this researcher's work—but that was of no use to Delia until she ascertained that this was, indeed, the Vickers line she sought.

"Maybe I'm doing something wrong," Delia said to the monitor. "Where's Roger when I need him? What other words can I possibly use to find a Web site about Jeremiah?" She needed a more unusual name or phrase, something that would eliminate from the search all the Petes and Jeremiahs that meant nothing to her.

When the light bulb finally went on over her head, Delia's enthusiasm was instantly renewed. "When all else fails," she muttered, "try the obvious."

She typed in *Jesus Creek, Tennessee*. Sure enough, there were only two listings. One was the town's official Web site, which Roger had already told her about. "Where did they find someone to create that Web site?" she asked the air.

The second page on the list stumped her. "Archives from an Arkansas newspaper?" With a genealogist's instinct, Delia clicked on that one and proceeded to scan the Web page that appeared. She had that tingle at the nape of her neck, the one which had so often before told her she was hot on the trail.

Halfway down the page was a short piece about a birthday party celebration for ninety-year-old Rosalie Hanks. Among those attending from out of town were Mary Gale Vickers nee Hanks and son, from Jesus Creek, Tennessee.

"Son!" Delia would have done a victory dance if her swollen ankle had allowed it.

She knew from past experience that she was about to pull an all-nighter. It was close to ten o'clock already, and here was a whole new world of possibility just opened to her. But first she had to share her discovery.

With her newly acquired skill, Delia sent another e-mail to Roger. *Have found a clue in the Vickers case,* she wrote, careful not to use all caps; Roger had warned her about that in his reply to her first note. *Will be surfing the Net for rest of night. See you for breakfast. Bring food.*

As soon as she'd sent the message, she realized just how long she'd have to wait for breakfast. What's more, she'd had no dinner and the hospital's lunch was only a dim memory. For the first time, she also realized that her eyes burned, her back ached, and all the bumps and bruises from the attack had returned to life.

She slowly raised herself on the crutches, then eased her stiff and battered body through the maze of books, folders, and miscellanea that lived with her. Coffee was essential; unfortunately she was down to the last spoonful, and it was clear that she'd need at least two pots to see her through the night. The rest of the cupboard was bare, too. Not a cracker or a rice cake to be found. The grocery stores were long closed.

And then she noticed through the window that lights were still on next door. Until then, she'd forgotten all about Lenny's funeral! Was it possible that some mourners still lingered in Lodina's house?

Delia pressed her face against the window, close enough to see that Patricia's car was still parked in Lodina's driveway. "There's food in that thar house!" she said cheerfully.

Taking just enough time to slip into a jacket, she made a clumsy exit through her back door, headed for Lodina's kitchen and a hearty meal. Certainly, she told herself, this isn't the time to question Lodina about her stepbrother. Unless talking would help take her mind off Lenny.

CHAPTER FOURTEEN

PATRICIA PATRICK OPENED Lodina's back door in response to Delia's timid knock.

"Why, Delia!" Patricia was drying her hands on a dish towel. No doubt she'd scrubbed the countertops, scoured the last of the casserole dishes and cake plates in preparation for returning them to their owners, and probably waxed all the floors for good measure. "Hon, I heard you'd been released from the hospital, but I just haven't had a minute to get over there."

"Don't worry about that," Delia told her. "Compared to what Lodina's been through the past few days, my injuries are a hill of beans. I came to check on her; I feel terrible about missing the funeral."

Patricia nodded her head. "It was a nice one, too. That Brother Wagoner preaches a good funeral, doesn't he?"

"Oh, yes," Delia agreed. "He always says just the right thing. Are you okay, Patricia?"

Patricia shook her head and chuckled. "Now, Delia, I know you mean well, but . . . well, don't you think that bump on your head might've addled you just a little? You don't honestly believe some crazy person is out to kill us all, now do you?"

Clearly Patricia was in good health, spunky as ever. And McClain's injuries, according to the nurse, were hardly life threatening. If it weren't for that bullet that Reb had dug out of her back porch, Delia might dismiss her own experience as nothing more than clumsiness.

Patricia didn't want to pursue the subject, however, and arguing would not get Delia any closer to food. "How's Lodina holding up?" she asked.

"Come on in the house," Patricia ordered, "before you fall off the steps. Should you be out and about? I'd think those crutches would sink right into this damp ground. If you aren't careful, you'll wind up back in a hospital bed before morning."

She ushered Delia into the too-warm kitchen, moving chairs and other obstacles out of the way to clear a path for Delia and her crutches. "Sit down there at the table," Patricia said, "and I'll fix you a plate. I know you're sick of hospital food."

"Oh, don't go to any trouble," Delia insisted, hoping Patricia wouldn't take her seriously. She eased her battered body into the nearest chair and tried to look famished. This didn't require great acting skills.

Patricia kept up a stream of chatter as she pulled covered bowls from the refrigerator. "You don't eat ham, do you? I don't know how you live without meat, Delia, I honestly don't. Well, there's a little bit of Roger's green beans left, and a dab of potato salad."

While Patricia loaded a plate with all the meatless leftovers she could find, Delia eased the conversation toward the subject she wanted to pursue. "Is Lodina still awake?" she asked hopefully.

"Yes, and the poor old thing is a mess of nerves." Patricia added a buttered roll to the plate and brought it to the table, along with flatware and a paper napkin. "She's in the bathroom splashing cold water on her face. I told her to take a nice hot bath, but she won't listen to a word I say."

"Well, she's always been stubborn," Delia agreed. "And right now we have to let her have her way."

"Such a shame," Patricia went on, shaking her head. "Lodina's the last one alive. That's got to be the loneliest feeling there is."

"But there's her stepbrother," Delia said. "Pete and Mary Gale's boy."

Patricia actually stopped talking for half a minute while the wheels turned. Finally she nodded slowly. "I haven't thought about that boy in a hundred years," she said. "I went to school with that Vickers boy. We all did. Now what was his name? He was real quiet, I remember, and never did much but sit in the back of the room. Hardly ever spoke. Sort of a sissy, for all his strapping size."

"I don't guess he's still alive," Delia pressed, "or he'd have been here for the funeral."

"Oh, I haven't got the foggiest notion as to his whereabouts," Patricia said. "Wouldn't you like a piece of Frankie Mae's chocolate pie?"

"Have you ever known me to turn down chocolate?" Delia contentedly finished her vegetables as Patricia bustled around, slicing pie and putting it on a plate.

Delia heard the click of the bathroom door as it opened, followed by Lodina's shuffling steps in the hallway. Pale and drawn, her appearance was no better than it had been the last time Delia had seen her. Still, Lodina's back was straight and her gaze steady.

"Delia," she said tonelessly.

"Lodina, hon!" Patricia hurried to her friend's side and, taking Lodina by the arm, led her to a seat at the kitchen table. "Now you sit down here. I'll fix you a glass of milk and I want you to take one of these nerve pills. Now don't argue with me, hon. You know you need a good night's rest."

"Yes," Lodina said, "I suppose I do."

"Lodina, I'm so sorry I missed the funeral," Delia apologized.

"Delia had a little accident," Patricia explained. She set the milk on the table in front of Lodina, then fished a small blue capsule from the bottle in her hand. "Now you take this."

Lodina reached out and picked up one of the crutches leaned against Delia's chair. "Is your leg broken?" she asked.

"It's just a twisted ankle," Delia said, playing down the seriousness of her injury. "I'm hopping around on those things for a while."

Lodina nodded.

"But since I couldn't do much else, I let Roger teach me to use that computer he gave me for Christmas. It's the most amazing thing. I can do all sorts of family research right there!"

"Oh, I've heard there's just awful filth on that World Wide Web!" Patricia cried. "You don't want to get involved in that, Delia. Haven't you heard the stories about women getting tangled up with perfect strangers and ending up dead?"

"Yes, but believe me, I don't plan to strike up an intimate acquaintance with anyone," Delia assured her. "What I like about it is the information. There are Web sites for just about every subject you can think of, including genealogy."

Delia tried to gauge Lodina's condition. Was it a good time to bring up the subject of her stepbrother? What would Miss Manners recommend?

Patricia solved the problem for her. "Is that where you came up with Bill Vickers?" she asked.

Lodina gave a half-laugh. "What on earth made you think of Bill Vickers?"

"It started with that old trunk I bought at the auction." Delia told them about Jeremiah's memoirs and her search for his connection to Pete Vickers. She was careful to leave out the part about meeting Jeremiah.

"Well, isn't that the strangest thing?" Patricia whisked the empty plate away from the table and replaced it with a slab of chocolate pie. "It's a shame we don't have a Vickers left anywhere in town to appreciate all this."

Delia turned and found Lodina staring back at her. "What do you think?" she asked. "Should we send Jeremiah's book to Bill Vickers?"

Lodina showed no particular interest in the subject. "I've never heard of this Jeremiah Vickers," she said simply.

"I think he must've been Bill's ancestor," Delia explained. "I'm sure any descendants would like to have this manuscript. It's full of details about Jeremiah's life, with some fascinating tidbits about the people in Jesus Creek back in the nineteenth century."

"Is it?" Lodina asked without interest.

"Whatever did become of that Bill Vickers?" Patricia asked.

"Did he stay on with you and your family after Pete left?" Delia asked. "Or did he go to California with his father?"

"Patricia," Lodina said irritably, "you've fiddled around here long enough. Go on home and get some rest."

"Hon, I'd hate to leave you right now," Patricia complained.

"I'll be fine," Lodina said. "I'll sleep soon. And Delia's here."

"Yes, but Delia's on crutches. She can barely get around."

"That's true, isn't it?" Lodina said. "All the same, I'll be fine. You run on now."

It seemed to Delia that Patricia was grateful to have been relieved of duty. And who could blame her? She'd run herself ragged ever since the day Lenny died. Patricia probably hadn't slept as much as Lodina had.

"Now you call me if you need anything," Patricia ordered as she scooted out the back door. "Anytime, however late."

"Thank you, Patricia." Lodina waved her friend off. "You've been such a dear."

As soon as the door closed behind Patricia, Lodina rose and took her half-empty glass to the sink. She poured the rest of the milk down the drain, then held up Patricia's nerve pill for Delia to see. "It's never a good idea to drug yourself," she said as she dropped it down the disposal. "So many things to watch out for, and drugs only cloud your mind."

"I can't disagree with that," Delia said, "but sometimes we have to give in, don't we? I mean, there are times when we have to surrender to the circumstances and take whatever help is offered."

"I don't need help," Lodina said calmly. She returned to the table and moved both crutches out of her way before sitting down. "I've always been strong, like my mother. And I do what has to be done."

"There's nothing left to do," Delia reminded her.

Delia understood how easy it was to get into the hectic rhythm that accompanied crisis. It had happened to Delia often enough—some unexpected emergency would blow the world apart and she'd run nonstop trying to collect the scattered pieces and glue them together again. When the predicament was over, she'd suddenly find herself still running full tilt, with no destination in mind.

"Just one or two things," Lodina said. "What is it you want

to do about Bill?"

"What do I want to do about him?" Delia asked. "You mean you know where he is?"

"I have some idea," Lodina admitted. "I've been waiting for him to make the first move. I gather he sent you in his place. He was a cowardly boy, so it shouldn't surprise me that he'd be a cowardly man."

Delia wondered if perhaps Lodina had taken something other than Patricia's nerve pill. "Do you want me to send Jeremiah's memoirs to Bill?" she asked, confused.

"You mean you haven't already? Why? Are you holding out for something from him? You'd be a fool to trust him. He was always a liar and a troublemaker."

Now Delia was completely puzzled. "Lodina, I haven't any idea—"

A solid rap at the front door startled them both. "Good heavens!" Delia said, and then, "Oh, it must be Patricia. She probably forgot something."

"Wait here," Lodina ordered. "I'll take care of it."

She scuttled away to answer the door, leaving Delia to muse about Lodina's peculiar behavior. Something was clearly out of whack with Lodina. Was it possible she'd actually lost her mind?

Delia recognized Dan McClain's voice. Why on earth, she wondered, was he stopping by to visit at such an hour? Then she realized with chagrin that she had done just that. All the same, she was stunned when Lodina led McClain into the kitchen.

"Delia!" he said. "What are you doing here at this hour?" His eyes were still red-rimmed, and minor burns were evident on his hands. Otherwise, though, Dan McClain seemed no worse for his experience.

"She's come to pay her respects." Lodina took her purse from the top of the refrigerator and dug in it for a handkerchief. "Like you. Now that we're all finally together, with some privacy, let's get down to business. What exactly do the two of you want?"

"Delia has nothing to do with our business. It's between

you and me, Lodina. Although I don't mind having a witness to the truth."

"Could somebody give me the background?" Delia asked. "Mr. McClain, Lodina buried her brother today. This isn't the best time to talk business. Obviously she isn't feeling well."

"Losing one's only family makes most of us feel bad," McClain said. "On second thought, I'm not sure that's true of Hemby women."

"I don't—" Delia began.

"They found him, you know," McClain said to Lodina. "Buried out behind the barn."

"So Delia has informed me," Lodina replied coldly.

"It's just a matter of time before the remains are identified."

"What do you think it'll matter?" Lodina asked. "You've already got the farm, for all that's worth. Pete Vickers didn't leave anything else."

"He left me," McClain said, looking straight at her. "He left an eyewitness to his murder."

Lodina paused to study his face. "Murder? I don't know what you're talking about!"

"What's going on here?" Delia demanded. "Lodina, what's he talking about? And Mr. McClain, what do you care about Pete Vickers—" Suddenly, understanding dawned. "Oh! You're Bill!"

"I haven't been Bill in a long time," he said, never taking his eyes off Lodina. "Not since the day I left here all those years ago."

"You ran off because you have no more spine than he had," Lodina said. "It's not my problem. You could have stayed and helped us run that farm."

"Hard to plow a field while looking over your shoulder. I was a kid, but I knew that much. I knew she'd kill me, too, the first chance she got."

"Who?" Delia asked. "What are you talking about?"

"Dot Hemby," McClain said. "My father's wife. The woman who killed him."

"That's nonsense," Lodina said. "Nobody would believe it."

"They will," McClain said confidently. "Because I can tell the whole story, and what I have to say will be confirmed by the autopsy. The shovel that smashed my father's skull left its mark. I can describe exactly what he was wearing and where he was standing when it happened. I can even remember what you were wearing, Lodina. His blood was smeared on your clothes, yours and your mother's."

"I burned those dresses," Lodina said, almost as an afterthought.

"You killed Pete Vickers?" Delia exclaimed. "Lodina, why would—"

"She didn't kill him," McClain corrected. "Her mother did. Dot was harping and nagging at my father, as she usually was. He was a peaceful man. Whenever Dot went off on a rampage, he'd just walk away, go into the woods. That's what he tried to do that day, but she stopped him. She picked up a shovel that was leaning against the barn, and she hit him with it. One good blow. And then her daughter came out and never flinched. Just calmly picked up the shovel and used it to dig the hole where they hid my father's body."

The purse Lodina had been holding slipped from her hands. It hit the floor, scattering coins, lipstick, and slips of paper across the kitchen floor.

Before the pennies stopped rolling, Lodina took two strides across the room and placed a gun against Delia's temple. "Patricia has the house so neat," she said, "I'd hate to mess it up. And besides, it makes more sense if you both die at Delia's. They'll think you shot her, then killed yourself."

McClain didn't move, just spoke quietly. "No one will believe it," he said.

"Sure they will," Lodina said confidently. "You're a stranger here. No one trusts you, they all suspect you're up to no good. And they'll find it's the same gun that was fired at Delia last night—and the same gun that killed Lenny, so naturally you'll be blamed for that, too."

"Lodina!" Delia didn't dare turn her head, but she couldn't help the exclamation. "You killed Lenny? Why? What were you thinking?"

"Because he asked me to do it, Delia." For the first time since McClain had arrived, Lodina seemed genuinely remorseful. "I loved Lenny. You know that's true. But he was dying. He had cancer, did you know that? No, he wouldn't have told you. He only told me, because we were that close. We kept no secrets. Well, except that one." She grinned at McClain.

"Lenny never knew what you and his mother did to my father, did he?" McClain asked.

"Why should he know? He wasn't there, he wasn't involved. And he didn't have the stomach for what needed to be done." Lodina practically snorted. "Only the women in my family are strong."

"But if he was dying anyway," Delia said, "why did you have to kill him?"

"I told you. He asked me to do it. He begged me, because he was afraid of what was coming. Lenny never could handle pain, not even a little headache. He knew it was best if he went quickly. And he knew I could be counted on to protect him, no matter what it took. It was the hardest thing I've ever had to do, but there was no choice. I understood that."

"Lodina." Delia spoke as calmly as she could under the circumstances, hoping to get through to Lodina's reasonable side. "There's a mistake. I've known you all my life. You're a good person, and you'd never—"

"There's no need to pretend, Delia. I knew you were in league with him"—she tossed her head in McClain's direction—"since that first night when you came in here, pretending to be so sorry for me. You started taunting me then, talking about the skeleton and asking about Pete. I didn't know how you'd figured it out, and then Bill came through the door. I should've recognized him at the auction, but it's been so long. I haven't even thought about Bill Vickers or his trashy daddy in all these years."

"Lodina, I wasn't taunting you. It's just a wild coincidence," Delia said. She didn't know why she bothered to argue. There was no way out of it now; both she and McClain knew that Lodina was responsible for one murder and for covering up another.

"Say what you like," Lodina told her. "I know you're both against me. But Mama raised me to take care of myself, without any help. Don't think because I'm old that I'm weak. Now let's get moving. I'd like to get a full night's sleep for a change."

"I'll need the crutches," Delia reminded her.

"You can lean on Bill," Lodina said. "That'll keep him busy. You should be glad. If he tries to stop me, I'll shoot."

Lodina carried the crutches but kept the gun close to Delia's head as the three of them hobbled across the yard. Never letting down her guard, she always stayed close enough so that neither of her hostages could make a run for it. Lodina, Delia observed, was an efficient and determined killer.

The overhead light in Delia's tiny kitchen was blinding after their trek in the darkness. "Lodina," she said, not daring to turn her head, "this is crazy. You didn't kill Pete Vickers, you only helped your mother bury him. You were a child. No one's going to hold you accountable for that."

"No one's going to know about it," Lodina replied. "Besides, there's still the problem of Lenny. Euthanasia isn't looked upon kindly in this country."

"You were devastated by his illness," Delia suggested. "Not mentally competent."

"That's the stupidest thing I ever heard." For the first time, Lodina's emotions got the better of her. "I'm not crazy."

"Of course you are," McClain retorted. "Sane people don't kill other people."

"Mr. McClain, if you don't mind," Delia said nervously, "I'd rather you not upset her while she's got a gun pointed at my head."

"What difference does it make?" McClain asked. "She's already told us we're going to die. What better time than now to tell the truth?"

"He's finally making sense," Lodina admitted. "Delia, I am sorry about you. I've enjoyed our friendship, and Lenny thought a lot of you. But you got involved of your own accord, so you have to take responsibility for it."

"It isn't Delia's fault, either," McClain said. "It's all you, Lodina. You're just like your mother. You want everything your way and you don't care who gets hurt, so long as your petty little desires are met. You're a psychopath. It runs in your family."

"And you're a pathetic, whimpering coward!" Lodina shot back.

"Haven't you ever wondered," McClain asked, "what became of your own father? I mean, Dot killed her second husband. Think she may have ended a spat with her first one the same way?"

"He fell off a horse," Lodina said. "Hit his head and died."

"Did you see that happen? Or is it just what your mother told you?"

Lodina bit her lip, considering the possibility that McClain had presented.

"Never occurred to you, did it?" McClain asked. "Did Delia tell you there's a second skeleton buried out behind the barn? Who else do you think your mother murdered and buried?"

Delia started to remind him that the second skeleton had been dead long before Dot Hemby was born, but McClain anticipated her argument. He tightened his grip on her arm to keep her quiet.

"Delia has to sit down," he said. "I'm putting her in the chair." Slowly, carefully, so as not to alarm Lodina, Dan McClain helped Delia hop the few steps to the dining portion of the kitchen. Putting both arms around her as if she were completely incapable of moving on her own, he eased her backward into a chair.

His face gave her no hint of what he had in mind, but Delia decided to go along with it. She followed his movement and allowed herself to sit. She glanced longingly at the computer on the table beside her. *Maybe*, she thought, *Roger will notice I haven't sent an e-mail lately. Maybe he's on his way here to find out why.*

As her bottom made contact with the chair, Delia felt

McClain's hand slide down her hip. Before she could register surprise, he grabbed one of the cables that dangled from the back of the computer and jerked it as hard as he could.

That cable, like all the others which fed life into the computer, ran across the floor and looped twice before plugging into the wall. It came flying toward McClain. On the journey, it slapped the back of Lodina's leg and caused her to look around instinctively, wondering what had attacked her.

McClain pounced, grabbing Lodina's wrist and forcing the gun to point up toward the ceiling, but Lodina was determined. She never let go of her weapon.

Delia watched the struggle with mounting horror. She saw the two of them fall to the floor. The gun continued to wave from side to side, up and down. Any second Lodina would wrest her arm free and kill McClain or Delia. She might even get them both with one shot!

Desperate to help, Delia grabbed the computer's keyboard and lurched forward, landing on her knees. The impact sent a string of pain shooting through her leg and down to her ankle, but Delia ignored it. The coiled cable which ran from the keyboard to the computer finally pulled loose, swinging around to smack Delia's cheek. She ignored that, too.

She slammed the keyboard down hard on Lodina's hand, smashing it time after time after time until Lodina cried out in pain, finally letting go of the gun.

McClain grabbed it and pushed himself away from his stepsister. Still on his knees, he pointed the gun at Lodina. "I stopped running away years ago," he said. "And I've got every reason in the world to kill you."

The strong and competent Lodina Hemby Lane burst into tears and begged for her life.

CHAPTER FIFTEEN

"I'D BEEN FISHING," Dan McClain said. "I'd caught a few that day, too. Thought we'd have them for supper. I was almost home, just a few feet to go before I came out of the woods, when I heard Dot yelling at my dad. I decided to wait until she'd cooled off before I went on home. And then I saw her murder him."

He'd given Reb the highlights, but now McClain shared the details with Delia and Roger. "I was barely fourteen years old and too scared of my stepmother and her family to speak up. Afraid I'd either be thrown in jail or even murdered and dumped in the ground beside my father."

Once McClain had subdued Lodina, Delia had called Reb at home. After that, of course, she'd called Roger. Both men had arrived together, neither bothering to cut their engines or even park their cars off the street.

Lodina had refused to speak a word. It fell to Delia and McClain to explain to the wide-eyed Reb what had happened. "I told you," had been the police chief's only comment. "I told you we'd hate it when we learned the truth about Lenny."

Even in handcuffs, Lodina had maintained an appearance of dignity. *A jury will have a hard time believing that she's a cold-blooded killer*, Delia thought. She hardly understood it herself. The cold reality of the last few hours was more dreamlike than her encounter with Jeremiah Vickers.

"But you didn't go to the police?" Delia asked, after McClain finished his story.

"Dot's cousin was the police chief," he answered. "That's a close-knit family. I knew that even if the law believed me, it would all be hushed up. Besides, Dot would have killed me.

I'm sure of that."

"What did you do? I mean, you were so young. How did you support yourself?"

McClain smiled. "That was a long time ago, Delia. Back in the olden days—just after the wheel was invented—a man-size boy could claim to be any age at all, and no one questioned it. I scraped by for a long time, lived in some unsavory places, and probably came within a hair of dying more than once. In the end, though, it worked out well enough."

Roger hadn't left an inch of space between himself and Delia since he'd arrived. Now he sat on the arm of the chair, his arm wrapped protectively around her shoulders. "I owe you an apology, Mr. McClain," he said. "For the way I acted that night outside Lodina's. I can see why you'd have hard feelings against the whole family. But Lenny really was a good man, you know."

"A good man, perhaps," McClain allowed. "Or a good actor. As far as I know, he never learned the truth about my father's murder. Most likely that's because he was out in the woods the whole time. He stayed there a lot."

A tiny smile crossed Delia's face. "He mentioned that he liked playing in the woods, camping there."

"Camping?" McClain asked. "Lenny's favorite pastime was catching rabbits and squirrels."

"Yes," Delia said. "He told me he used to stay out for days, catching his own food and—"

"He didn't eat the animals," McClain told her. "He just cut off their legs, one at a time. Then he'd put them out and see how far they could get before he cut off the next limb. Lenny found it entertaining to watch them try to escape."

Memoirs of Jeremiah Vickers, chapter 46, page 618

"It's no wonder he wanted the robbers captured," I said to Miss Clarissa. "Bad enough to bear the burden of acts he did perform. And yet, I cannot help but wonder—was he, indeed, the abominable outlaw of lore, or the kindly, God-fearing man we knew?"

"Mightn't he have been both, Jeremiah?" she asked, with a

gentle hand upon my arm. As always, her innate intellect had sifted the possibilities and what remained was the truth without prejudice.

We grieved not for the thief and killer Jesse James, but for the good friend J. D. Howard. As I meditated upon the hardship of such a life as he had chose and upon the torment inside that must have bothered him every moment, I took my only comfort in the words he spoke that night: "The only peace an outlaw finds is in the grave."

AUTHOR'S NOTE

The beginning of the end

On the afternoon of September 7, 1876, eight men rode into the quiet town of Northfield, Minnesota, intent upon robbing the First National Bank. Being seasoned veterans of the outlaw trade, they had every reason to believe this job would be as successful as all their others.

In the past, the James-Younger gang had been the thorn in the side of local lawmen as well as the Pinkertons. The gang's ability to escape from even the most elaborate traps set for them bordered on the supernatural.

Some say the Jameses and Youngers had eluded the law in the past because they had the support of their neighbors. Folks who knew—or knew of—the boys believed the former Confederate soldiers were fighting back against injustices perpetrated against them and their families by the Union aggressors. During the war, Jesse and Frank's family had been stripped of their home; their stepfather had been beaten, strung up, and left to hang by Union soldiers; and their female relatives had been imprisoned for the crime of being related to Confederate soldiers.

Neighbors and friends who had suffered similar fates were sympathetic when the James boys appeared to be taking revenge on the banks and railroads which were controlled by carpetbaggers and the Union government. Many figured Jesse and Frank were getting even with the Yankees, and these folks were all too willing to aid and abet the Jameses.

Others say those neighbors kept quiet because they were afraid of swift and merciless retribution from Jesse and

Frank James.

The people of Northfield, Minnesota, were neither sympathetic nor frightened. At the cry of "Robbery!" merchants and residents of the small town hauled out their weapons and, for all intents and purposes, put an end to the glory days of the most famous outlaws in American history.

Young Nicholas Gustavson was shot and killed by one of the escaping robbers. Gustavson was a recent immigrant from Switzerland who barely spoke English. He probably died without ever understanding what all the commotion was about.

Bank employee Joseph Heywood told the robbers that the safe was on a timer and could not be opened. Showing his spunk, Heywood fought back by slamming Frank James's hand in a desk drawer.

As the robbers made their escape from the bank, one of them killed Heywood with a shot to the head. It was cold-blooded murder, and the identity of the killer has never been confirmed.

Northfield's losses were tragic, but the town had dealt the outlaws a devastating blow. Bill Chadwell and Clell Miller died in the street. Miller's body was later put on display at events throughout the state.

Charley Pitts and the Youngers—Bob, Cole, and Jim—rode off into the woods along with Frank and Jesse James. Jim took five bullets in the shoulder; Cole was shot in the side and thigh, collecting a total of twelve bullet wounds before it was done; and Bob Younger, the most seriously injured, ended up with a broken elbow and a bullet in his lung.

Lost in unfamiliar territory, and with four of the six members in increasingly bad shape, the gang hobbled through the backwoods, slogged through creeks and rivers, and even holed up on a swampy island until finally deciding to split up. Since Jesse and Frank were uninjured and could travel faster, they rode off together. This left the Youngers and Miller to struggle along as best they could. (There are stories that claim Jesse suggested killing the seriously injured Bob Younger to give the rest a better chance of escape. Cole

Younger, who had no great love for Jesse, never made this claim, however.)

After two weeks of relentless pursuit, the Northfield posse caught up to the injured men, and Clell Miller died in the shootout which followed. Admitting defeat, the Younger brothers surrendered and were sentenced to prison terms.

Frank and Jesse James were never captured, but the disastrous Northfield raid had taken its physical and emotional toll. Apparently the James boys were convinced that the time had come to turn their lives in another direction.

Rumors and tales and vaguely remembered incidents concerning the mysterious Mr. J. D. Howard

In the spring of 1878, Mr. and Mrs. J. D. Howard arrived in Waverly, Tennessee. They put up for a few days at the Nolan Hotel (now the Nolan House Bed and Breakfast) prior to renting a farm from W. N. Link in the nearby community of Big Bottom.

The Howards were popular with their new neighbors, often hosting dances and barbeques at their home. J. D. Howard, a "fairly good-looking fellow" (the ladies in the Big Bottom described him as "the best looking man in the county") with dark brown whiskers and blue eyes, was always respectful and courteous toward the ladies. He was known to play poker, but he generally lost; and when he thought others were cheating at the game, he came down hard on them. Howard did not tolerate cheaters.

Mrs. Howard was an excellent cook and a compassionate woman who often tended the ill. The Howards attended Bowen's Chapel Cumberland Presbyterian Church, and Howard sometimes preached the service when called upon to do so. No doubt the ladies in Big Bottom were on hand to console the Howards when their twin sons, Gould and Montgomery (named for the doctors who delivered them), died shortly after birth.

The men of Humphreys County considered Howard a good enough sort, although they nicknamed him Rabbit Man because of his timidity. Certainly they respected his skill as a horseman. Howard was an avid racer, and even laid out a racetrack on the farm he rented. His favorite mount, a sorrel called Red Fox, was nearly unbeatable in a race.

Still, there were certain incidents which did not fit with the timid personality.

J. D. Howard never tied his horse to a hitching post. Instead he would pay some child a penny to hold the reins. Riveted to his saddle were two large pistol holders. Some of the war veterans recognized it as a guerrilla saddle. When asked, Howard explained that the saddle had been outfitted that way when he bought it. Certainly he had no use for holsters, he reminded them, for even though he carried a couple of guns in his saddlebags, he didn't like weapons and never expected to use one.

Howard suffered a bout of malaria shortly after he arrived in Humphreys County. Maybe it was the lingering effects of his illness combined with the smoke-filled, stuffy air in the local saloon which caused him to faint.

In any case, when he hit the floor, Howard's coat fell open, revealing to the concerned onlookers a pistol in a shoulder holster. Upon being revived, Rabbit Man immediately reached for his gun . . . then quickly covered it again with his coat.

A disagreement over the outcome of a horse race prompted Howard to tell his rival jockey, "You'd be dead now if I hadn't promised Zee." Sudden flare-ups of temper such as this one convinced a wise few that Howard was no rabbit.

For almost two years, Mr. and Mrs. J. D. Howard lived good if ordinary lives in Humphreys County. And then, with no word or warning, they were gone. Howard left behind some pending court cases—most of them related to unsettled debts, so perhaps the neighbors thought he was running from creditors. Perhaps he was.

No doubt others were surprised that Howard would renege on a debt. Henry Harris, the station agent, had loaned him money when the Howards first arrived in Humphreys County. Howard had made a point of paying back the loan.

Folks in the Big Bottom community probably speculated

about the odd habits and sudden disappearance of the mysterious J. D. Howard. It's a safe bet, though, that not one of them came close to guessing the truth about the Rabbit Man or his motives.

Housework may be hazardous to your health

April 3, 1882. Robert and Charles Ford had been guests in the St. Joseph home of Jesse and Zee James for quite some time. They were not there on a friendly visit, however. Bob and Charlie Ford were looking to collect the reward for killing Jesse James.

A justifiably paranoid man, Jesse always went armed, never turned his back on anyone, and was smart enough to distrust even close friends. The Fords had definitely outstayed their welcome, according to Zee, but they were determined to make a quick buck through the murder of their old friend and gang leader.

On this morning, after enjoying a hearty breakfast served by their hostess, the men were talking in the front room of the small house. According to Bob Ford's testimony, Jesse suddenly removed his pistols and climbed on a chair to dust a picture frame.

Taking advantage of the rare opportunity, Bob Ford drew his pistol and fired a single shot into the back of Jesse's head. By the time Zee James ran into the room, her husband was dying. He spoke no final words.

Or maybe it happened this way . . .

As a young man, before the war took him in another direction, Jesse James had considered becoming a preacher like his father. Especially after the disaster in Northfield, he was tired of the outlaw life and wanted only to settle down, raise his children, and grow old alongside his beloved Zee.

Banks and railroads wanted him dead. Hundreds of others, including most of his former gang members, wanted the $10,000 reward. It was obvious to Jesse that the only peace an outlaw finds is in the grave.

And so Jesse James faked his death.

He lived to a ripe old age, went by a multitude of aliases, and fathered a tribe of children.

In the end. . .

Charlie Ford committed suicide a few years after the death of Jesse James.

Bob Ford was killed ten years after murdering Jesse. His killer was Ed Kelly, who had a hankering for Bob's woman.

Bob Younger died in prison. His brothers Jim and Cole served their sentences (they were model prisoners) and lived out their lives in relative peace.

Frank James turned himself in to authorities, was tried and acquitted of all charges against him. He lived until 1915, supporting himself and his wife, Annie, with a variety of legitimate jobs.

Zee James lived hand-to-mouth until her son, Jesse Edwards James, was old enough to help support the family. Jesse Edwards became a highly respected lawyer and judge, although he was generally the prime suspect in any local crime, simply because of his family background.

Ancestors of Jesse Woodson James

Generation No. 1

1. Jesse Woodson James, born September 05, 1847, in Kearney, Clay Co., MO; died April 03, 1882, in St Joseph, Clay Co., MO. He was the son of 2. Robert Sallee James and 3. Zerelda Cole. He married (1) Zerelda Amanda Mimms on April 23, 1874, in Kansas City, MO. She was the daughter of John W. Mimms and Mary James.

Generation No. 2

2. Robert Sallee James, born July 17, 1816, in KY; died August 18, 1850, in CA. He was the son of 4. John James and 5. Mary Polly Poor. He married 3. Zerelda Cole on December 28, 1842, in KY.

3. Zerelda Cole, born January 29, 1825, in Butler Co., KY; died February 10, 1911, in Kearney, Clay Co., MO. She was the daughter of 6. James Cole and 7. Sallie Lindsay.

Children of Robert James and Zerelda Cole are:

    i. Alexander Franklin James, born January 10, 1843, in Kearney, Clay Co., MO; died February 18, 1915, in Kearney, Clay Co., MO; married Annie Ralston in June 1874 in Kansas City, MO.

More About Alexander Franklin James:
aka: B. J. Woodson
Fact 5: served with Quantrill's Raiders

    ii. Robert B James, born July 19, 1845, in Kearney, Clay Co., MO; died August 21, 1845, in Kearney, Clay Co., MO.

1 iii. Jesse Woodson James, born September 05, 1847, in Kearney, Clay Co., MO; died April 03, 1882, in St. Joseph, Clay Co., MO; married Zerelda Amanda Mimms on April 23,

1874, in Kansas City, MO.

    iv. Susan Lavenia James, born November 25, 1849, in Kearney, Clay Co., MO; died March 03, 1889; married Allen Parmer.

Generation No. 3

    4. John James, born 1775 in VA; died 1827 in Logan Co., KY. He was the son of 8. William James and 9. Nancy Mary Hines. He married 5. Mary Polly Poor on March 26, 1807, in Goochland Co., VA.

    5. Mary Polly Poor, born 1790; died 1827. She was the daughter of 10. Robert Poor and 11. Elizabeth Mimms.

    Children of John James and Mary Poor are:

    i. Mary James, born September 28, 1809; died July 23, 1877, in Kansas City, MO; married John W. Mimms in 1827.

    ii. William James, born September 11, 1811; married (1) Mary Ann Varble; married (2) Mary Ann Gibson Marshall.

    iii. John R. James, born February 15, 1815; married (1) Amanda Williams on September 01, 1836, in Logan Co., KY; married (2) Emily Bradley 1872.

  2 iv. Robert Sallee James, born July 17, 1816, in KY; died August 18, 1850, in CA; married Zerelda Cole on December 28, 1842, in KY.

    v. Elizabeth James, born November 25, 1816; died November 01, 1904, in Mountain Grove MO; married Tillman West.

    vi. Nancy Gardner James, born September 13, 1821; died Abt. 1875; married George B. Hite.

    vii. Thomas Martin James, born April 08, 1823; died December 25, 1903; married Sarah Woodward.

    viii. Drury Woodson James, born November 14, 1826; died July 01, 1909; married Louisa Dunn.

    6. James Cole, born September 08, 1804; died February 27, 1827, in fall off horse. He was the son of 12. Richard Cole and 13. Sally Yates. He married 7. Sallie Lindsay.

7. Sallie Lindsay. She was the daughter of 14. Anthony Lindsay and 15. Alsey Cole.

Children of James Cole and Sallie Lindsay are:
      i. Jesse Richard Cole, born November 29, 1826; married Louisa Maret.
   3 ii. Zerelda Cole, born January 29, 1825, in Butler Co., KY; died February 10, 1911 in Kearney, Clay Co., MO; married (1) Mr. Simms; married (2) Robert Sallee James on December 28, 1842, in KY; married (3) Reuben Samuel on September 12, 1855.

Generation No. 4
8. William James, born Abt. 1754 in Pembrokeshire, WALES; died 1805. He was the son of 16. Thomas James. He married 9. Nancy Mary Hines on July 15, 1774 in Hanover Co., VA.
9. Nancy Mary Hines, born in ENG.

Children of William James and Nancy Hines are:
   4 i. John James, born 1775 in VA; died 1827 in Logan Co., KY; married Mary Polly Poor on March 26, 1807, in Goochland Co., VA.
      ii. Nancy Ann James, born February 24, 1777; married David Hodges on December 21, 1796.
      iii. William James, born April 27, 1782; died 1807; married Drusilla Horner.
      iv. Robert Thomas James, born December 14, 1783 in VA; died in Yellow Creek, Dickson Co., TN.
      v. Henry James, born Abt. 1787 in TN or VA; died July 30, 1873 in Washington, Hemstead Co., Arkansas; married (1) Catharine Evans; married (2) Martha Browne.
      vi. Martin James, born Abt. 1789; married Elizabeth Key.
      vii. Mary James, married Edward Lee December 22, 1796.

10. Robert Poor, born June 18, 1763 in Goochland Co.,

VA; died 1801. He married 11. Elizabeth Mimms.

11. Elizabeth Mimms, born April 03, 1769. She was the daughter of 22. Shadrack Mimms and 23. Elizabeth Woodson.

Children of Robert Poor and Elizabeth Mimms are:
    5   i. Mary Polly Poor, born 1790; died 1827; married John James March 26, 1807 in Goochland Co., VA.
       ii. Martha Patsy Poor.
     iii. Drury Woodson Poor, born December 07, 1787.
     iv. Robert E. Poor, born 1792.
      v. Elizabeth Poor, born July 21, 1795.
     vi. Nancy B. Poor, born 1796.
    vii. James Poor, born 1797.

12. Richard Cole. He was the son of 24. Richard and 25. Ann Hubbard. He married 13. Sally Yates.

13. Sally Yates.

Children of Richard Cole and Sally Yates are:
    6   i. James Cole, born September 08, 1804; died February 27, 1827 in fall off horse; married Sallie Lindsay.
       ii. William Yates Cole, born September 17, 1788.
     iii. Mary Polly Cole, born 1792; married Elijah Finnie.
     iv. Elizabeth Cole, married Thomas Martin.
      v. Sally Cole, born July 24, 1807.
     vi. Jesse Cole, born May 21, 1793.
    vii. Amos Cole, born February 1798.

14. Anthony Lindsay. He married 15. Alsey Cole.

15. Alsey Cole.

Child of Anthony Lindsay and Alsey Cole is:
    7   i. Sallie Lindsay, married (1) James Cole; married (2) Robert Thomason in 1838.

Generation No. 5
    16. Thomas James, born Abt. 1717 in Montgomery Co.,

PA; died Abt. 1788. He was the son of 32. John James.

Children of Thomas James are:
    i. Samuel James.
    ii. Josiah James.
    iii. Isaac James.
  8 iv. William James, born Abt. 1754 in Pembrokeshire, WALES; died 1805; married Nancy Mary Hines on July 15, 1774, in Hanover Co., VA.
    v. Aaron James, born Abt. 1775; died in Yellow Creek, Dickson Co., TN.

22. Shadrack Mimms, born 1734; died 1777. He married 23. Elizabeth Woodson on May 24, 1760.
23. Elizabeth Woodson, born Abt. 1734. She was the daughter of 46. Robert Woodson and 47. Rebecca Pryor.

Children of Shadrack Mimms and Elizabeth Woodson are:
  11 i. Elizabeth Mimms, born April 03, 1769; married Robert Poor.
    ii. Robert Mimms, born June 29, 1764, in Goochland Co., VA; died Abt. 1828 in Goochland Co., VA; married Lucy Poor on April 06, 1788.
    iii. Mary Mimms, born June 18, 1766.
    iv. Sally Mimms, born July 1771.
    v. Martha Mimms, born January 17, 1774.
    vi. Susannah Mimms, born June 24, 1776.

24. Richard, born 1729; died November 21, 1814 in Midway KY. He was the son of 48. John Cole and 49. Susanna. He married 25. Ann Hubbard 1762.
25. Ann Hubbard.

Children of Richard and Ann Hubbard are:
  12 i. Richard Cole, married Sally Yates.
    ii. John Cole, married Nancy Hines.
    iii. Jesse Cole, married (1) Nancy Sparks; married (2) Elizabeth Roberts; married (3) Elizabeth Hyatt.

iv. Rachael Cole, born 1760; married Willa Jett.

v. Betsy Cole, married Mr. Snape.

vi. Agnes Cole.

vii. Sallie Cole, married Benjamin Graves.

viii. Alsey Alice Cole, born June 20, 1769; married Anthony Lindsay, Jr.

ix. Lucy Cole, married Jonathan Cropper.

Generation No. 6

32. John James, born in Pembrokeshire, WALES; died 1726 in Bucks Co., PA.

Children of John James are:

16 i. Thomas James, born Abt. 1717 in Montgomery Co., PA; died Abt. 1788.

ii. William James.

46. Robert Woodson, born Abt. 1708 in Henrico Co., VA; died September 19, 1750, in Goochland Co., VA. He was the son of 92. Benjamin Woodson and 93. Sarah Porter. He married 47. Rebecca Pryor.

47. Rebecca Pryor, born Abt. 1704; died 1748.

Children of Robert Woodson and Rebecca Pryor are:

23 i. Elizabeth Woodson, born Abt. 1734; married Shadrack Mimms May 24, 1760.

ii. Mary Woodson.

iii. Sarah Woodson.

iv. Benjamin Woodson.

v. Robert Woodson.

vi. James Woodson, born Abt. 1734.

vii. John Woodson, born 1739.

48. John Cole, died 1757 in Culpepper Co., VA. He married 49. Susanna.

49. Susanna, died 1761.

Child of John Cole and Susanna is:

24 i. Richard, born 1729; died November 21, 1814, in Midway, KY; married (1) Ann Hubbard 1762; married (2) Emsey Margaret James July 21, 1795, in Woodford Co., KY.

Generation No. 7

92. Benjamin Woodson, born 1666 in Curles Plantation; died August 1723 in Henrico Co., VA. He was the son of 184. Robert Woodson and 185. Elizabeth Ferris. He married 93. Sarah Porter on July 12, 1700, in Henrico Co., VA.

93. Sarah Porter, born Abt. 1668; died Abt. 1722.

Children of Benjamin Woodson and Sarah Porter are:

46 i. Robert Woodson, born Abt. 1708 in Henrico Co., VA; died September 19, 1750, in Goochland Co., VA; married Rebecca Pryor.

   ii. William Woodson, born 1700.

   iii. Benjamin Woodson, born Abt. 1702.

   iv. Joseph Woodson, born 1704.

   v. John Woodson, born 1706.

   vi. Sarah Woodson, born Abt. 1710.

   vii. Elizabeth Woodson, born Abt. 1712.

Generation No. 8

184. Robert Woodson, born 1634 in Fleur de Hundred, VA; died 1707 in VA. He was the son of 368. Dr. John Woodson and 369. Sarah Winston. He married 185. Elizabeth Ferris in 1656 in Curles Plantation.

185. Elizabeth Ferris, born in Leicestershire, ENG.

Children of Robert Woodson and Elizabeth Ferris are:

92 i. Benjamin Woodson, born 1666 in Curles Plantation; died August 1723 in Henrico Co., VA; married Sarah Porter on July 12, 1700, in Henrico Co., VA.

   ii. John Woodson, born 1658; married Judith Tarleton.

   iii. Robert Woodson, born 1660; married (1) Sarah Lewis; married (2) Rachel Watkins.

   iv. Richard Woodson, born 1662; married Ann Smith.

v. Joseph Woodson, born 1664; married Mary Jane.

vi. Sarah Woodson, born 1668; married Edward Moseley.

vii. Elizabeth Woodson, married Wiliam Lewis.

viii. Judith Woodson, born 1673; married William Cannon.

ix. Mary Woodson, born 1678; married George Payne.

Generation No. 9

368. Dr. John Woodson, born 1586 in Devonshire, ENG; died April 19, 1644, in Jamestown, VA. He married 369. Sarah Winston.

369. Sarah Winston, born 1590 in ENG; died in VA.

Children of Dr. Woodson and Sarah Winston are:

184 i. Robert Woodson, born 1634 in Fleur de Hundred, VA; died 1707 in VA; married Elizabeth Ferris 1656 in Curles Plantation.

ii. John Woodson, born 1632 in Fleur de Hundred, VA; died 1684 in VA; married Sarah Browne.

BOOKS ABOUT JESSE JAMES

Brant, Marley. *Jesse James: The Man and the Myth.* Berkley, 1998.

Highley, Robert E. *Jesse James Though Officially Dead Lived On For 65 Years.* Maverick.

Love, Robertus. *The Rise and Fall of Jesse James.* G. P. Putnam's Sons, 1926.

Settle, William A. *Jesse James Was His Name.* University of Nebraska Press, 1966.

Steele, Phillip W. *Jesse and Frank James: the Family History.* Gretna. Pelican Publishing Company, 1991.

Steele, Phillip W., with George Warfel. *The Many Faces of Jesse James.* Gretna. Pelican Publishing Company, 1995.

Yeatman, Ted P. *Frank and Jesse James.* Cumberland House, 2000.

WEB SITES

The Old West, plainview.com/lace/law.htm

Desperado, www.geocities.com/Heartland/Plains/4743/outlaws.html

The James-Younger Gang, www.islandnet.com/~the-gang/

Jesus Creek, www.JesusCreek.com

Library HQ, www.libraryhq.com (Click on *Site Source*)

SETI at home, setiathome.ssl.berkeley.edu/

Jesse James Lived and Died in Texas, freepages.history.rootsweb.com/~ivyplace

Refuting the Courtney-James Claim, home.earthlink.net/~ariannayoungblood/

Jesse James Virtual Museum, www.jessejamesvirtualmuseum.com